"Memory"
Survival

Peter G. Casazza and
Janet C. Tremain

Copyright © 2023 Peter G. Casazza and Janet C. Tremain
All rights reserved
First Edition

PAGE PUBLISHING
Conneaut Lake, PA

First originally published by Page Publishing 2023

ISBN 979-8-88960-048-0 (pbk)
ISBN 979-8-88960-059-6 (digital)

Printed in the United States of America

Contents

Foreword v
1. Rude Awakening 1
2. Saving Signal 8
3. Noodling 16
4. Turkey-Coq 25
5. Hunting Memory 33
6. Wooden Canoe People 40
7. A Walking Encyclopedia 46
8. Disk Shot 53
9. Outrunning a Bear 62
10. Eidetic Memory 71
11. A Hunter's Life 82
12. Chinking 89
13. Horsing Around 96
14. Weird Wednesdays 106
15. Dying by Suicide 113
16. The Fugitive 120
17. Swollen Up 129
18. The Toothbrush Fairy 134
19. Joining Forces 140
20. Dodging Danger 148
21. Nothing Is as It Seems 157
22. The Beginning 164

Foreword

This murder mystery/love story is built around the unlikely survival of a female genius and a brilliant stranger. The heroine of the book has hyperthymesia and an eidetic memory, which allows her to remember every single moment of her life since she was one year old and everything she ever saw or read. Of the eight billion people in the world, perhaps only twenty-five have this.

The female heroine, Memory, is based on the author, Janet Tremain, who has these traits. That is why this book is very different from any book you have read. While weaving your way through the mysteries, you will learn more incredible facts about the world than you could ever have imagined. And you will find out that much of what you think you know is not actually true.

1

Rude Awakening

Oh no! What is happening? I am covered in blood, flat on my back on the ground, facing a log cabin. There is a male leopard appaloosa horse gently nuzzling me that seems to have woken me up. He is white with dark spots, tall, and his back and side are covered in blood. He doesn't have a saddle or bridle. I have no idea who he is or where he came from.

The saddlebags I usually carry on my bike are right next to me. My clothes are damp. I must have been passed out for quite a while. The sun is blinding. I can barely open my eyes. There are oak trees to the left of the cabin. I also see a firepit near my head. Could this be a dream? Nothing is making any sense. How can I check if this is a dream? Lucid dream experts claim that familiar things will not be normal in a dream. Here's my compass watch. Are the numbers in the right order? Yes. Here's my hand. The fingers look normal. Why are my hands bloody? What has happened? Where in the world am I?

My watch indicates fifteen more minutes have passed. I must have passed out again. I was lying here all that time. Am I alone? My head really hurts! I have a large gash on my forehead. There is a bloody firepit rock next to me. I must have fallen off that unknown horse and hit my head on the rock. I have a splitting headache, and I've never had a headache before. They think it is because I produce more adrenaline than most people. My ears are ringing. This must be some sort of concussion.

More time has passed, and I'm still on the ground. Everything appears slightly out of focus. I'm dizzy. I don't think I can stand up. My left buttock is killing me. Did I fall on something sharp? Let me roll on my right side. Nothing sharp here. I have two holes in the seat of my pants. Oh no! There are also two holes in my left buttock. These must be through and through bullet holes. There's a lot of blood. Who would have shot me, and why? Are they still around here?

I need to get into the cabin as quickly as possible and think. I will have to crawl into the cabin. Luckily it is only eight feet to the door. I will crawl two feet and then drag the saddlebags with me. They are extremely heavy, and they shouldn't be. Everything is such an effort. Crawl. I am at the front porch to the cabin, but it is one foot high. Put both arms on the porch and drag myself halfway onto the porch. Lifting the saddlebags onto the porch is excruciatingly painful. Just drag myself forward one more time to get to the door. Drag the saddlebags. I am at the door. Seems like it took forever. I can barely get my arm up high enough to open the door. It has a latch instead of a doorknob. Luckily, it opens inward. Now crawl inside with the saddlebags and close the door.

I can't seem to remember how I got here. Do I know my name? Coral Holmes comes to mind. How'd my saddlebags get here? What is the horse doing here? My head really does hurt. I am going to have to lie here and rest. The cabin is one room with a wood floor. There are bunkbeds to the right with a three-rung ladder to the top bunk. The left wall is all shelves with the first half filled with books and the far end empty. Against the far wall is a wood cooking stove with a pile of wood to its left. To its right is a cabinet with a small basin, which does not have running water but drains out back of the cabin. It's just a plain wall to the right of the basin and beyond the bed. To my right at the end of the bed is a row of clothes hooks and in the corner a broom and dustpan. In front of the stove is a table and four chairs.

I cannot remember what happened. I seem to have lost my short-term memory. I don't know how I got here or why. I have no idea who shot me or why. Am I in imminent danger? I seem to have my long-term memory. This is the cabin my grandparents used as a summer home for years. I would spend summers with them. We would hunt, fish, bird-watch, cut firewood, and they had me read every day.

Time seems to have stabilized a bit. I still don't think I can stand up. Unfortunately, I have blood on my sneakers, pants, and shirt. It will be hard to get the blood out of my clothes, but that is the least of my worries right now.

There is my bed on top. There are four words written on the wall above my bed in felt-tip permanent marker: *hyperthymesia and eidetic memory*. Oh yeah. These conditions lead to people being able to remember an abnormally large number of their life experiences, books, things they have seen on TV, or articles they have read and in vivid detail. I can remember my whole life since I was at most fourteen months old as if it were yesterday. It is extraordinarily rare, with fewer than one hundred people in the world having been diagnosed with these conditions. The word *hyperthymesia* comes from the Greek words *thymesis*, meaning "memory," and *hyper*, meaning "excessive."

My grandparents told me I have that, so they called me Memory. My memory is like a library of VHS tapes, DVDs, and live-streaming videos, walk-throughs of every day of my life from waking to sleeping. My memory is running movies that never stop. I see the world in "split screens," with the past constantly playing at the same time as the present. It is extremely difficult to concentrate since every event encountered is running parallel to my memory of historical facts and other related memories. It is so strange to have one day of my memory missing now.

Stay awake! I always keep instant coffee and water bottles in my saddlebags. I need to get them open. Just chug some grounds. Ugh! That is really bitter and disgusting. Chew some more. Drink some water to wash down the grounds. Here are some EpiPens. These might be useful. Oh, that's right, they are for attacks of angioedema. That is a swelling that is similar to hives, but the swelling is mostly under the skin instead of on the surface.

I have had a problem with this my whole life. This is not a dream. It is all too real.

Under the clothes hooks is Grandfather's old walking stick and a fruit crate. The fruit crate was my chair when I was little. Let's try to stand up. Ugh! Painful! Unfortunately, I don't carry aspirin, and I have terrible pain all over. I need to do something with these two bullet holes and my head gash to prevent infection.

What did my grandparents teach me about first aid and survival? Willow bark is the basis of aspirin, and chewing it relieves pain. It is called "salicin," from the Latin name for the white willow Salix alba. This has been known throughout history, and it is often referred to as being used for pain during the time of Hippocrates, although the historical record does not exactly support this. Overuse of willow bark even contributed to the death of Beethoven. There goes my split-screen memory. I have never been able to stop my historical memory from interfering with the present, but I am at least used to it now.

My grandparents once had me read a survival book that described how to treat wounds in the wilderness. Pine trees ooze resin when they're damaged. The resin has antibacterial properties, which protect the damaged tree from getting infected. Pine sap is also anti-inflammatory, and its stickiness helps it protect wounds. In ancient Greece and Rome, doctors also used spiderwebs to make bandages for their patients. Spiderwebs supposedly have natural antiseptic and antifungal properties and help promote clotting. But I don't see any large spiderwebs in here. Also, I read that you need to clean the skin around the wound, don't stitch it so pus can come out, and clean it every day. This is where a good memory really pays off.

There is still no memory of why I'm here or why someone shot me. I may have retrograde amnesia! This usually comes from head trauma and disturbs short-term memory but leaves long-term memory intact. This must have happened from my falling off the horse and hitting my forehead on that bloody rock outside.

For now, I need to go and find some willow bark and pine sap. Take another swig of water. I can probably walk with the aid of the walking stick. I need to be careful. I am very unstable. It is difficult just making it out the front door, and my buttock is killing me while I walk. It is really bright out here, even squinting.

"MEMORY" SURVIVAL

"Hello, horse. I have no idea who you are, so I'm just going to name you Horse. I'm surprised you're still here. I guess you are as confused as I am as to what happened. There is a fenced pasture one hundred yards downhill southwest from here. The pasture is an acre of land which is about the size of a football field. On its left is an Osage orange grove, and to the right is a group of pussy willows. I might as well take you to the pasture on my way to the pussy willows. Between the walking stick and holding onto your mane I can probably make it. This trail used to be worn down to dirt. Now it's covered in tall grasses. To my right is a group of pine trees, and to my left is a large overgrown garden area followed by a pawpaw patch. Pawpaws are the Missouri state fruit trees. Slow down, Horse. I can barely hold on.

"Along the path, there are always dozens of squirrels. In the summer I would come every day and feed the birds and squirrels nuts and seeds. After a while they would come as soon as I arrived. Those were wonderful days. The bird songs are louder than I recall. We've made it to the pasture. You like me talking to you, don't you, Horse?

"The fencing is made of Osage orange trees tightly woven together while just saplings. My grandparents planted these fifty years ago when they came here in the summer with packhorses and built the cabin. Osage orange intertwines its branches and has sharp spikes, so it was used to fence in animals before barbed wire was invented in the 1870s. Sorry, Horse. I have no control over my memory. It just blends in with reality. This pasture is covered in grasses that are safe for you to eat.

"There is a spring in your pasture which drains downhill to the right into a creek. There are over 4,400 springs in Missouri, including Big Spring, one of the largest springs in the United States, and you have one of them, Horse. The spring water is very clear. My grandparents somehow fixed this two-inch PVC pipe to direct the spring flow out far enough from the vertical embankment so collecting water is easier. What a fresh taste this water has.

"First, I will splash some of this spring water on my face and buttock to clean the wounds. I have to go, Horse, so I will close you in with the wooden gate."

The pussy willow-type tops of the willow shoots are right here. My Swiss army pocketknife will easily cut slivers of these. Peel the shoots a little and cut some pieces. Now, just slightly chew and swallow the juices. Remember to spit out the woody parts after a while. I will put extra pieces in my pocket for later pain.

Now for the pine sap. There was a pine forest on the way here. I will hobble back toward the cabin until I get there. This is incredibly strenuous. Here are some pine trees on my left growing too closely together. There are already some injuries from deer antlers, so sap is oozing out. Deer rub their antlers on the tree to remove antler velvet and to establish territory. This grove is overcrowded, so if I endanger a tree, it may be for the better. No container to use. I should tie up my shirt and rub some of this pine sap on my belly. I will have to leave my knife open for now. It is a good thing my head wound is on my forehead and I have a ponytail, so I won't get sap in my hair. This sap will work fine for my wounds. Good. Now we'll trudge back to the cabin and treat these wounds. This walking stick is really helping, but it seems like forever getting to the cabin. It's a miracle I made it.

The willow bark is finally helping with the pain, so spit the wood pulp outside. Now, put the pine sap on my left forehead, and smear some sap on the two holes in my left buttock. I keep ace bandages in my saddlebags for exercise injuries. I can use the scissors on my pocketknife to cut off strips to cover the wounds. The sticky sap will hold them on. Now for the leftover sap on my belly. Carefully scrape it off with my knife, wipe it on a shelf, and put a piece of bandage on my belly. I will have to leave my knife open on the table.

That was all extremely tiring. I still can't remember anything from today. I better write down today's events on a notepad so I can check my memory tomorrow. I have notepads and pens in my saddlebags.

Woke up on the ground in front of cabin, gash on forehead, two bullet holes in buttock, horse and saddlebags next to me, blood all over my clothes, struggled to get into the cabin, no short-term memory, took horse to the pasture, daylight was blinding, chewed willow bark, birdsongs were too loud, dizzy, and put pine sap on my wounds.

"MEMORY" SURVIVAL

I have an upset stomach, so eating is out of the question. Let me take off my wet shoes and socks and put them on the table. I am completely exhausted and should go to bed. These rope beds are made of thick nylon rope crisscrossed back and forth in both directions. They form a box spring of sorts.

My memory again. Nylon was invented by DuPont in the 1930s. They were used for women's stockings, or "nylons," in 1940. During World War II, almost all nylon production was diverted to the military for use in parachutes.

There is a feather-stuffed cloth mattress. Also, there is a thinner feather-stuffed comforter and a pillow in trash bags to keep them clean. The top bunk was mine when I was here with my grandparents, but now I can sleep on the bottom bunk.

I am glad this day is over. It was a complete nightmare. I hope tomorrow I will have some idea what happened. For now, just close your eyes and forget everything, if possible.

2

Saving Signal

Woke myself up screaming. What was that nightmare? I'm drenched in sweat, and my heart is pounding. Someone was chasing me with a gun and trying to kill me. Just a faceless frightening figure who came out of nowhere. I was running from building to building on some college campus. Gunshots everywhere but kept missing me. Then I woke up. This dream probably came from the fact that I've been shot. When dreaming, you firmly believe what's happening is real. Thank goodness that is over. Do I have a fever? Drink some water. My face seems to be the same temperature as the water bottle. It was just a nightmare.

It's already sunrise. I must have slept twelve hours. My wounds have really taken a toll on my energy. It's so quiet in here, no city noises. I'll open the shutters. The cabin has thick wooden shutters on each side of the door. Each is in two pieces and open in. There are screens instead of glass windows. The roof over the porch keeps the rain out.

My head and buttock are killing me. In a lot of pain. Let me chew some more willow bark. I still have no idea what happened yesterday or why someone would shoot me. Where did Horse come from? Why am I at my grandparents' cabin? I'm in some kind of trouble. I need to know if I'm in imminent danger. Let's check my short-term memory since yesterday. Take the notepad and record what happened yesterday.

Now compare it to yesterday's list. They are identical, so I have my short-term memory since yesterday. Good. I guess I am stuck with instant coffee straight from the jar. Take a drink of water. I can't make a fire in the stove since I don't have matches or even a mug, and I'm too tired to think of alternatives.

Right now I need to go to the outhouse. It's only twenty-five yards northwest of the cabin, but it will be a difficult twenty-five yards. Luckily, I see a roll of toilet paper on the shelf. Head out the front door with Grandfather's walking stick. Wow! The birds are almost deafening. They seem so happy. I guess anyone would be happy if they could fly, and I certainly wish I could fly right now.

Keep putting one foot in front of the other, and you will get there eventually. My grandparents have not been here in three years, so almost anything could be living in the outhouse. I must be careful. The door is stuck, and I barely have enough strength to yank it open. Looks empty, but to be safe, I will leave the door open. There is a wooden bench with a hole. Fine. There is a bucket of lime and a scoop. Dump a scoop of lime in the hole and close the door as I leave to keep critters out. Going back to the cabin is just as exhausting. It seems like a small miracle that I made it back.

I have no food, but I keep two protein bars in my saddlebags. Let me look in the saddlebags. I don't understand. I have eight bottles of water and eight protein bars. Drink a lot of water. I also see rolls of gauze, duct tape, my favorite salad dressing of oil and balsamic vinegar, my favorite sheep cheese, peanut butter, a headlamp with extra batteries, a cloth backpack, and a change of clothes. Let me put this stuff on the shelves. This is really strange. I never carry this much stuff in my saddlebags. Why would they be here now? This looks more like a travel kit. Was I running from something? Let's eat two protein bars and drink some water.

Let me open the other side of the saddlebags. There is a rain suit in a small pouch, a ziplock bag with a toothbrush, toothpaste, dental floss, and a comb. There are also some manila folders of my work. There are Faraday bags in here.

Here comes my parallel memory-intervening universe crowding in. Modern payment cards have a built-in chip that transmits the cards' information wirelessly. Today, a person just has to walk past you on the street with an RFID (radio frequency identification) skimming device, and it will steal your ID information directly from debit and credit cards, smartphones, tablets, and even laptops. It can also intercept your electronic car fob. Michael Faraday was the father of electromagnetism and invented the Faraday cage in 1836, which became the Faraday bag of today. Faraday bags are to protect electronic devices from skimming.

Inside the Faraday bag is a wallet, cell phone, and my car fob. Since I put my cell phone in a Faraday bag, I must be trying to hide from someone since this bag blocks GPS from tracking your location. The cell phone is turned off so the battery will last six months. Here's a wallet. Yes! This wallet does belong to Coral Holmes, so I do know my name at least. Let me put this stuff away. Put the ziplock bag with toiletries next to the basin and the rest of it on the shelves. I can put the saddlebags under the bottom bunk.

My grandparents always left a bottle of whiskey here when they left at the end of the summer. If it was gone or opened, they would know that someone had been here. There's the whiskey bottle. Wait a second. It is one-third empty, and there is a note with it: "Sorry! Got stuck here in a storm. Here is a $10 bill. Hunter."

Hey, $10 bill, You are going to test my long-term memory. In 1861 the two sides of the Civil War issued the first paper currency in the US to help fund the war. In 1862, the $2 bill was introduced but never caught on because it was considered bad luck. The National Banks Act after the Civil War introduced a government monetary system where banks issued paper notes. This led to two thousand different paper currencies, and people had trouble telling if they were authentic or if the bank was sound. The Federal Reserve Act of 1913 created a national banking system that could keep up with the changing financial needs of the country. The Federal Reserve Board then issued the first federal note in the form of a $10 bill. The oldest modern-world currency is the British pound at 1,200 years old.

Someone has been here, so I need to lock the door. My grandparents installed a barn door lock that consists of two U-shaped metal plates screwed into the wall on both sides of the door, and a two-by-four drops down into the slots to make an unbreakable entryway. They put the same locks on the shutters. Now I feel a little safer. I wonder who was here. They were at least polite. Now I can put some whiskey on a piece of gauze to clean the sap off my knife and my belly. I'll put my knife back in my pocket.

I desperately need to get my short-term memory back. I do have my long-term memory, so I know that I have a joint appointment in the Computer Engineering and Mathematics departments at the University of Missouri (MU). But if I ran, it means the danger may be there, so I cannot contact anyone until I know who I can trust.

When my grandparents left at the end of the summer, they buried all the pots, pans, utensils, etc., from the cabin so they would not be stolen over the winter. They also buried some food separately. I should go dig this stuff up. Let me open the door and step outside.

Listen! That is definitely a rabbit screaming. It must be in mortal danger since rabbits do not have vocal cords; this is why they are so quiet. They relay danger to each other by thumping with their strong back feet. They only scream when in extreme danger by exhaling air straight from their lungs so hard it sounds exactly like a child screaming. I need to get there fast but certainly can't run yet. A fast walk will have to do.

The rabbit is still screaming. I can hobble at best. Faster! I am almost there. There is a swamp rabbit in the creek and a coyote trying to kill it. The coyote is about two feet tall and around thirty pounds. He has grayish-brown fur, large triangular ears, a long narrow muzzle, and a long bushy tail. He turned his head, and his black nose and yellow eyes are aimed straight at me. He is growling and showing his fangs.

Normally, a coyote would run away, but this guy is hoping to have rabbit for lunch, so he has decided to stand and fight. A hungry coyote is quite aggressive and very dangerous. I've spent years in martial arts training and will use these skills. I will give him a major front kick by coming up under his white belly. That sent him three feet into the air. That hurt me more than it hurt him. It worked. When he landed back on the ground, he ran off yelping. Sometimes adrenaline comes in handy.

Why does this make me feel like I have killed someone? It feels real, but I don't believe I would ever kill anyone. I can't worry about it now.

How's the rabbit? Oh no. He is grinding his teeth. For a rabbit, that means he's in pain. I see. He is holding his right front leg up. It may be broken. He will never survive out here. I think it is a male, but it is difficult to tell without a closer look.

"Hey, little swamp rabbit. What are you doing here? You guys are mostly in southeast Missouri. You are a long way from home. You are going to be just fine. I'm going to talk to you calmly before I gently pick you up and fix your leg back at the cabin. You are a good bunny."

Normally you could not catch a rabbit in the wild. They are incredibly fast. But this guy is seriously wounded and can't run. I will have to grab him up before he can react. Quick grab with two hands around the belly, and I've got you! Oh, this is a juvenile male swamp rabbit. Swamp rabbits are the only rabbits that swim regularly. I need to hold him so his feet are pointed away from me, or he will use his powerful hind legs to kick my chest hard enough to get out of my hands.

"I'm taking you to the cabin, little fella. It would help if you did not keep squirming around while we walk to the cabin. But you are just doing what comes naturally to a captured rabbit. At least you've stopped screaming. We are finally here in the cabin. You really tired me out. This might hurt a bit, little fella. I'm just wrapping your hurt leg with some gauze. Around and around with the gauze, but not too tight. I'll have to hold it on with duct tape. You'll be as good as new in a month or so. You need a name. How about Signal, since your ears pick up signals and you signaled me with your lung scream?

"Let me look at you, Signal. Your ears are about four inches long, stick straight up, and they seem to rotate about a hundred and eighty degrees. I know you like to be close to water and hide in tall grasses until your night foraging. You look similar to cottontail rabbits. What a cute head and back you have, with all of the browns, rusty red colors, black-and-white hairs sparsely here and there. Your eyes seem to be lined with a cinnamon coloring. Your tail, chin, and belly are white. You are beautiful, or should I call you handsome?

"I'll put you on the floor to the right of the basin in the corner. Let me grab the fruit crate and rip off a couple of the wooden slats to make a house for you. You'll feel safer and protected with a house you can hide in. Signal, there is an old folk song my father used to sing to me:

> Rabbit ain't got no tail at all, tail at all, tail at all. Rabbit ain't got no tail at all, just a powder puff.
>
> Same song, second verse, could be better, but it's gonna be worse. Rabbit ain't got—

"Signal, you are just thumping and thumping. I guess you don't like my singing. Everybody's a critic today. Stay here while I get food for you. What would you like to eat? Some dandelion greens and wild strawberry leaves. I will eat the strawberries. I will also get the same greens for me.

"Let me go out and get us some food."

*****

"Signal, I'm back. Here are some greens I found in front of the cabin. You are hiding in your house. Good, Signal. I did not find your favorite timothy hay. You probably just want to rest at the moment. I will have some water, a protein bar, and use my knife to cut some cheese. I am exhausted from saving you, so I'll take a nap with you. I'll sleep on the bottom bunk again."

Wow. I was in a deep sleep for an hour. Feels good. I needed it.

"Signal, I am up. You'll be fine. Just rest. I am going out again for a while, and it will be quiet in here. Try not to chew on your duct tape."

I should dig up the box of metal objects first since I need a bowl for Signal's water, utensils, and a coffee mug. To bury treasures, the spot must be easily found by memory, but don't pick an obvious spot.

The package must meet three criteria: watertight, structurally sound, and compact as possible. Do not put metal items in with other items as robbers may use a metal detector to locate them. My grandparents twice wrapped the stuff in trash bags, put them a wooden box, and then wrapped the box twice in painter's plastic sheeting. We buried them a foot deep and applied pepper spray to deter animals from digging them up. I can bring my backpack and a bottle of water. There is a shovel under the porch. Here's the shovel. Let's get busy. "We're burning daylight," as Grandpa would say.

My compass watch indicates this is north. Walk off twenty paces west and ten paces south. Luckily, the dirt is somewhat soft since I don't have a lot of strength. But this is still going to be strenuous. Each shovelful is painful, but I have to fight through it since I will run out of food soon. Luckily, my years of martial arts training have left me very strong. Dig. Rest. Dig. Rest. Maybe I will lie on my back a few minutes and rest. We have beautiful clouds today. There are cumulus clouds that look like fluffy white cotton balls in the sky. The high ice clouds are cirrus clouds. These are delicate, feathery clouds that are made mostly of ice crystals. There are also stratus clouds hanging low in the sky as a flat, featureless, uniform layer of grayish gold. Birds are singing all around.

I can only spare thirty minutes. I think I fell asleep again. I need to finish digging. There's the box. I don't have the strength to carry it back to the cabin, and it would take a lot more digging before I can lift it out. So I will open it here. My knife will cut open the plastic sheeting, and the shovel will pry the box open. Cut the inside trash bag, and I can carry the contents to the cabin in multiple trips. In the first trip I will put the metal coffee mugs, metal plates and bowls, and a carving knife in the stockpot in my backpack. I can carry the cast-iron skillet and the axe in my hands. Remember to talk quietly to Signal. He is already terrified. The walk back to the cabin is on the diagonal of a right triangle, and so it is only twenty-two paces. This is short and relatively quick.

"Signal. We have stuff. Here is a bowl of water. You must be thirsty. I will leave this stuff on the table for now since I have to make another trip."

"MEMORY" SURVIVAL

Another short trip back to the hole. This time, I can take the saucers, kettle, cooking and eating utensils, a carborundum stone, a first aid kit, an old crystal radio, cotton balls, petroleum jelly, and a roasting pan I can use to carry them. That empties the box. I will leave the hole open since I hope to be out of here soon and can then refill the box before I leave. Along the way I will gather up some acorns under the oak trees next to the cabin and put them in my backpack. I am glad this is the last trip. This is all the energy I have left.

"Signal, I am back for good. Now we have some kitchen supplies. All this work has brought back my pains. I feel like I have been beaten up. We keep aspirin in the first aid kit. Yes, here it is. But I don't see any antibiotic ointment. Not good. I need to put the acorns into the stockpot with water. The ones that float have to be thrown out since they are rotten inside. Now use my knife to cut open the acorn shells and put the meats back into the pot. If I remember, the next box contains cloth flour sacks. I can put the acorn meats into a sack, and the next time I go to the spring, I will take the sack and soak it in the water to get the tannins out. They will be ready to eat in a day."

That digging has worn me out. I don't have the strength to dig up the other box, although I need food. This will have to wait until tomorrow. I'll have to eat peanut butter, a protein bar, and cheese for dinner. Keep drinking lots of water. That is all I can take for today. I have to go to bed. First thing tomorrow morning, I must dig up the box of food and other stuff. I still have no recollection of what happened. I need to get my memory back. I may be in great danger but don't know exactly why. Let me put the bar on the door and close the shutters.

Get on the bunk. It feels good to lie down. I am so tired I will fall asleep quickly listening to the tree frogs singing and some locusts' rhythmic buzzing sounds.

3

Noodling

Had another nightmare last night. I was pedaling my bike as fast as I could because someone was chasing me in a car trying to run me down. I swerved, and it almost hit me. The chase went on and on. I was terrified. Finally, it was catching up, so I ran my bike into a river to get away since no one drives their car into a river. Dreams seem frighteningly real. I'm drenched in sweat again.

"Signal, you need to stay in your house and rest today. You had quite a traumatic experience yesterday. Here's your greens and water. I still can't make a fire so I will have protein bars and a salad for breakfast since I have my favorite salad dressing, utensils, and plates. Dissolve some coffee grounds in a mug of water. This cold coffee is terrible, even in a mug of water. Let me clean my wounds with whiskey since it kills bacteria and wards off infection. It burns like fire. Put on new pine sap. I absolutely must get more food today. I better dig up the second box right now."

Grab the shovel and my backpack and head out the door. It is bright and sunny. Not surprising since the average temperature in June is seventy-five degrees. This time we go twenty paces east and ten paces north. Here's the spot. The ground is soft again. Not as bad as yesterday since I'm slowly regaining my strength. It's hard to believe that I used to spend an hour a day vigorously practicing martial arts and lifting weights. Digging is still strenuous. I have made it halfway down to the box. Maybe I will sit and take a rest.

"MEMORY" SURVIVAL

It is fun watching the squirrels chasing one another up the trees, out on the branches, jumping to the next tree, and scrambling down. There's so much life all around. Scampering squirrels, singing birds—no city noises at all. Such beautiful, peaceful sounds. Even the rustling of the leaves in the breeze is soothing.

That's enough rest. I can finish digging now. I see the box. I'm still not strong enough to lift it out of the hole, so I will again cut the plastic sheeting with my knife, pry the box open, and cut the inside trash bag. We have a lot of good stuff: bar soap, towels, toilet paper, candles, matches, string, cloth bags, and trash bags. I'll stuff these in my backpack. There are also two collapsible water jugs I can carry in my hands. Again we are only twenty-two paces from the cabin. It is much easier walking today. That was an easy trip. I'll put this stuff on the table for now and move them to the shelves later. Take a drink of water.

"Signal, we have stuff, but I have to make another trip. Be right back."

Quick trip to the hole. The squirrels have already found it.

"Get out of here squirrels. This is my stuff."

I see foil, ziplocks, dried vegetables, spices, oatmeal and rice in labeled mylar bags that keep food fresh for twenty-five years. There is instant coffee, which luckily stays at full flavor for twenty years. This will fit in my backpack. This empties the box. I'll leave the hole open for now. I may want to save the boxes later. Short trip to the cabin. Signal is moving around a little better even if it is only on three legs. I can put all this stuff on the shelves. At least I have some food. Even though I'm not 100 percent yet, I'm getting better.

Since I now have matches, I will make a small fire in the upper firebox and have my first hot cup of coffee and some hot oatmeal. Let me first check the flue and make sure it's not clogged. Looks fine. There is plenty of firewood to the left of the stove.

"Signal, you might just as well learn. Take cotton balls, flatten them, and squeeze petroleum jelly into the balls until they are soaked. Even though petroleum jelly contains petroleum, it doesn't burn. But when you light the cotton balls, the cotton ball begins to act like melted wax. The liquid petroleum then starts boiling and giving off gas. This gas then burns. The cotton ball will give off a steady flame as long as it is saturated with liquid petroleum."

I will get this started in the oven. I can put a kettle of water on the stove and oatmeal in a bowl. I already put instant coffee in a mug, so it just needs water. The water is hot, so I can put some in my mug and the rest in the oatmeal. It is great to finally have a hot mug of coffee. The oatmeal has set. A normal meal for a change. Easy cleanup in the basin. This was exhausting. Signal is out of his house. I think I will lie on the floor for a moment, so Signal can see me. I am drowsy. I might just take a short nap. Oh no! I can't breathe. What is wrong? Am I having a heart attack?

"Signal. Why are you sleeping on my chest? I can barely breathe. We don't know each other that well. You must have liked the warmth. You shouldn't be moving around so much. Thanks for waking me up. Signal, this cabin was built by my grandparents fifty years ago on land passed down through generations to my grandmother. Everything was brought in by packhorses. They used a chainsaw to cut the logs. We have one of the few log outhouses anywhere.

"Hey, Signal, you are my only student now, so I might as well share my memory overload with you. Who do you think invented the chainsaw? People think it was invented by woodsmen, perhaps in Oregon. Before Cesarean sections, there were a number of mothers and babies who died in childbirth as the baby got stuck in the birth canal. They used a knife to cut through the pelvic bone to release the baby. This was called a 'symphysiotomy.' But this took well over an hour, and by then, mother and/or baby might die. The solution was a prototype of the chain saw invented in 1780 by two doctors. It was powered by a hand crank and had teeth on a chain that wound in an oval and was designed to more quickly cut through bone. The precursor to today's chain saws was developed in 1830 by two OBGYNs. You can store that in your long-term memory, Signal.

"Signal, I am tired, but I must get more protein, or I will end up roasting insects. So I will get a catfish in the creek. Catfish are very interesting fish. Catfish can be found all over the world in freshwater and saltwater. They get their name because of the catlike whiskers coming out of the sides of their face. Catfish have one hundred thousand taste buds! The male sea catfish carries the fertilized eggs in their mouths until birth. Finally, catfish do not have scales. They have smooth skin since they breathe through their skin."

Put the acorn meats in a flour sack and tie it closed. I can take the sack to the spring, fill the water jugs, and get more pine sap. I'll need to bring my backpack and put in it the big sharp knife, five ziplock bags, a piece of string, and a trash bag to carry some moss in. First I will sharpen the knife with the carborundum stone. I will carry the water jugs in my hands. I need to know if anyone has been here while I am gone, so I will put a small leaf in the crack of the door on the hinge side. If someone opens the door, the leaf will fall down, and I will know they were here.

The walk to the creek is fun. You can watch the squirrels and listen to the birds. They always seem so happy. I see a long stick along the path to use in my quest. Horse is at the other end of the pasture. I will put the bag of acorn meats in the spring and use another piece of string to tie it to a rock so it does not float away. Fill the water jugs. I will leave them just outside the gate and pick them up on the way back. Get some pepper-tasting watercress, plantain and dandelion greens, and put some moss in a trash bag for Signal.

Here are some puffball mushrooms to cook with the fish. They are huge white smooth balls and taste wonderful. I can put a few in ziplock bags. I see some morel mushrooms. It is the beginning of June, which is the very end of early morel mushroom season. There are nineteen species of morels in Missouri, some growing from April to September. You have to avoid the fake red morels. Cut the morels lengthwise to be sure they're hollow. The rule is this: "If they're not hollow, don't swallow." Then discard the stems. Put them in a ziplock bag, and put all these bags in my backpack.

With any luck there will be protein today. It's going to be tricky to catch a catfish since I don't have a fishing pole. Grandfather often said, "If you are in the wild and only know one way to do things, you are at a serious disadvantage." So I'll use catfish noodling to get a fish, even though noodling is illegal in Missouri. My grandparents showed me how to catfish noodle.

This creek has changed a lot since I was here last. There are still clusters of cattails along small portions of the bank, and they are filled with redwing blackbirds squawking as they lift their red-striped wings with each song. I will cut some cattail pollen tops and put them in a ziplock bag. The shape of the creek has changed somewhat as the clear water flows over large flat stones and deposits silt here and there. I guess it is continuously changing over time. Groupings of pebbles migrate, becoming smaller until nearly sand in some spots where the water trickles over them sparkling in the sunlight. Floating leaves and small twigs pass by until entrapped on the pebbles in places for a while, before breaking free and continuing their journey. An occasional water spider hitches a ride on a leaf. Do they care where they are going? Clumps of deep mud along the banks seem fixed and undisturbed by the current; mud where catfish and turtles could be hiding.

Catfish bury themselves in the mud near the bank. I need to go into the water and poke my stick in the mud to determine whether the mud nests contain a snapping turtle or a catfish. It is going to be difficult but worth it. If you can locate them in the mud, you can actually grab them with your hands and lift them out of the water. Experienced noodlers poke their stick into the mud and can feel the difference between a catfish, a snake, or a turtle. If the stick says it's a catfish, you can jam your hand in the hole and grab the catfish. Sometimes you can do this without putting your head underwater, but sometimes, you'll have to take a deep breath and submerge yourself.

Quietly and carefully poke the stick in any mud nests along the bank. No luck. Keep going. Wow! I didn't think it would be so hard to find a catfish. Finally, this one is soft, and I can tell from the way the stick is wiggling this is a catfish. Now for the hard part. Catfish have lots of tiny dull hacksaw-like teeth. It is going to hurt at least a little. Watch out for the sharp dorsal fin. Here goes my hand. Yikes! We're definitely deep into a catfish mouth. Put my hand all the way in and through the gills. Now pull it up. It's not too big. This one is fighting me, but I have a strong grip on it.

"MEMORY" SURVIVAL

Get it onto the bank. My hand got scraped, but it will be okay. At least the dorsal fin did not get me. That would really hurt. Great. I'll cut the head off the fish so there is no pain. Then use water to wash it and use the sharp knife to fillet the meat off along the dorsal fin. Careful not to puncture the guts. I will put the fish fillets in a ziplock bag in my backpack and throw the remains in the creek. Head back to the cabin and grab the full water jugs along the way.

Now stop at the pine tree grove and scrape pine sap onto my belly. A short trip back to the cabin. Take out the leaf. Don't forget not to scare Signal. I will have to use soap to wash my hands in the basin so they don't stink. Scrape the pine sap onto the shelf and use some whiskey to clean my knife and belly.

"Signal, I got spring water for your bowl. Also, some moss for your bed so you will have known smells. Moss is sometimes yellow but turns green with the introduction of moisture. You can eat it, but bunnies only eat moss if they are starving. Let me grab a few twigs just outside the cabin for you to chew on. Your teeth continually grow, and you have to regularly chew hard objects to keep them at their proper length."

I'll have to cook the fish and mushrooms in the outside firepit so I don't disturb Signal. It has a grate. Bring out some wood from next to the stove. Arrange. This time, I can use some pine sap to start the fire since it is highly flammable. Shouldn't take long to have a good fire. I will leave the skin on the fish filets and score it since it will come loose during cooking.

The fire is ready. We'll steam the fish, morels, and puffballs with some salt and thyme seasoning. Put everything in the skillet, add a little water, cover it in a foil tent, and put it on the grate. There. I will put my wet sneakers and socks next to the fire to dry. I will also put a kettle of water on the grate for coffee. I have a spare set of clothes on the shelf. Let me take off these wet bloody clothes and soak them in the basin. Then I can drape them over the chairs so they can dry. Unfortunately, it it is almost impossible to get blood out of clothes.

Hungry! Everything is cooking in the skillet. That's good. I can't wait. I'm starving. It looks ready. Use a towel to carry the skillet indoors. Let it cool a bit. Now dig in with this fork. The skin just breaks away. Yum. It's great. I needed that. The mushrooms are tasty.

The water is hot. Sprinkle some instant coffee grounds in the mug and add water. Maybe some carbohydrates will help me think. I can use the cattail pollen. The pollen was used in the olden days for flour to make pancakes and more. Put the pollen in the stockpot, mix in some water until we get a thick, stiff dough. I will wrap it around this green stick in a spiral and squeeze it with my hands so it does not fall off. The mixture is yellow. Just sit here and hold the dough over the slowly dwindling fire coals. Good enough! Just eat it straight off the stick. Tasty and nourishing. Then again, I could eat just about anything right now.

The temperature has suddenly dropped, and the sky looks threatening. June is still tornado season in Missouri. Tornados often appear later in the day as the sun is approaching the horizon. The sky has a greenish tinge, and the wind is getting strong. Under a thundercloud the sky is green due to scattering by water droplets within the cloud. When blue objects are illuminated with red light, they appear green. I better bring my sneakers, socks, and everything else inside.

Listen to the crystal radio with the earphones to find out what is going on. Oh no! We are under a tornado warning. This is serious. A tornado watch just means "Be prepared," tornados are possible. A tornado warning means "Take action," a tornado has been sighted or indicated by weather radar. I need to fasten down the window shutters and get prepared. There are hints that a tornado may form. Sudden drop in temperature is one. The formation of mammary clouds is another.

Here goes my memory again. Missouri is home to the most destructive tornado in US history. The tristate tornado, which set down on March 18, 1925, was a category five tornado with wind speeds between two hundred and three hundred miles per hour. This is the maximum damage rating issued on the Fujita scale.

It killed at least 751 people, injured 2,298 others, and demolished an estimated fifteen thousand homes throughout Missouri, Illinois, and Indiana. Annapolis, Missouri, was 90 percent destroyed.

Go outside. There is something called "flash to bang method," which tells you how far away you are from a lightning strike. Just count the number of seconds that pass between a flash of lightning and the thunder that follows. If five seconds pass, the lightning is one mile away; ten seconds equals two miles, fifteen seconds equals three miles, etc. There is also a rather-strange way to tell if rain is coming. Pinecones open and close depending on the humidity to help their seeds disperse. When the weather is dry, the pinecone opens so wind can catch the seeds and spread them. When rain is coming, the pinecone closes to prevent the seeds from escaping and becoming waterlogged.

"Signal, we have no place to hide. I will get under the bed, and you can get in your house. My knee caused a floorboard to pop up. There is a letter under the floor made out to me. I will have to read it later. I hope the tornado does not come through here. Horse can hide under the large Osage orange trees. At least we are on the side of a mountain and in the woods. This is not a guarantee of safety, but it makes it less likely we'll be hit.

"There is a myth that you should open the windows during a tornado to let the wind blow through. Actually, this just causes the wind to weaken the internal supports and can cause the house to collapse. The wind is shaking the cabin. What a mess. The shutters are rattling. Signal, you are thumping and thumping. I know you are scared. You think I am making this racket and are demanding that I stop. The hail on the roof is deafening. It sounds like a dozen people pounding hammers on the roof. This must be what it sounded like when they put on the shakes. We will know if a tornado is coming as it will sound like a freight train barreling down on us.

"Seems like forever. There, it has clearly passed. We are safe. Let me open the shutters and let some cool, fresh air in. I should go outside to see if we have any damage to the cabin. I'll be back."

I don't see any damage. They are a few small tree branches on the roof, but they can stay there. Horse is out in his pasture and seems fine. There are branches all over and a couple of small trees down. Otherwise, we seem to have survived. I don't want to go too far since there is mud everywhere and I'm barefoot. Might as well go back in the cabin. I will use a towel to clean off my muddy feet and the mud on the floor. I should open the envelope. There is a safety deposit box key in here and a letter from my parents and grandparents. It reads as follows:

> Memory, since you are always scurrying all over the cabin, we left this under the floorboards, hoping you will find it as a treasure. The safety deposit box key is to box number 137 at the Missouri Credit Union. In there is your inheritance. You will get it either when you get married or when you turn 25. We love you very much. Mom, Dad, Grandma, Grandpa.

Let me put the letter on the shelf. I wonder why my grandparents did not tell me about this. I will have to ask some time.

"Signal, it is time for bed. Here is some food and water. Let me lock the shutters and door. We've had a really big day and are very weary. See you in the morning."

4

Turkey-Coq

"Good morning, Signal. Here's some water and greens. I will use the last of the wood for the stove to heat water for coffee and oatmeal."

Wash up, brush teeth, comb hair, and clean my wounds. The water is hot so I can eat breakfast of oatmeal and hot coffee. That was good. I need to cut some wood for the stove. Take the axe and go out the door. Oh my. What a wonderful gift viewing the sunrise is. The trees are in silhouette as the sun barely peaks over the horizon as a bright yellowish glare reflecting shades of pinks, purples, oranges, and yellows onto the few lower-hanging clouds in the sky. As the sky transitions from grays to blues, the sun's brightness increases slowly. Just think, this happens every day.

My grandparents keep several cords of wood covered by tarps next to the cabin, but the pieces are too large for the stove. I'll have to split the big pieces into four smaller pieces. There's a stump here. Just set a log upright on the stump and split it down the middle with the axe. Be very careful. If the axe bounces off the wood, it could hit my leg with devastating results. Here is the first cut. Next, split each of the two pieces in half. Now they are ready for the stove. I should split at least fifteen pieces of cordwood so they will last a couple of weeks. This is quite tiring since I am still a little weak. It will take several trips into the cabin to pile up half of it next to the stove.

"Signal, the first covering of the gable roof was just sod laid on plastic sheeting and had to be watered. Later my grandparents used a horse-drawn wagon to bring shakes for the roof and screens for the windows to keep bugs out. Contrary to some popular beliefs regarding log-cabin building, logs were not fitted together as tightly as possible. The wood expands or contracts with variances of heat and moisture from season to season, so space was left between them for this process.

"One of the final steps was chinking to fill in the gaps between logs to keep out the weather, insects, vermin, and snakes. A wide variety of materials was used for this process. My grandparents used clay and mud. This has to be replaced over time, and my grandparents worked on it every summer. One summer, they brought a wood-burning cookstove by putting it on a wagon and having one of the horses pull it. They had a rustic road built from I70 south of here to within one mile of the cabin. A four-wheel-drive vehicle can make the trek now.

"After my parents died, my grandparents reared me. My grandparents were both schoolteachers and had summers off, so we came here every summer. The books you see on the shelves are because they had me read a book a day to increase my knowledge. I still remember every book I read as if it were yesterday. I stopped coming here eight years ago when I went to graduate school. My grandparents stopped coming here three years ago as they were in their eighties. I have really missed this place."

I definitely need to get something more to eat. That fish was small. I need more protein. So I will hunt a turkey today.

My memory again. Turkeys originated in North America over twenty million years ago. In the 1500s, the Spanish first encountered the turkey in the Americas. They thought turkeys looked like peacocks and so named them *pavos*. The turkey was then brought to Turkey from America. It was shipped by merchants in the east, mostly from Constantinople, to England. Thus, an American bird got the name *turkey-coq*, which was then shortened to "turkey."

To hunt, I need to make a primitive bow and arrows. Here is where my memory really pays off. Horse's fence is made of Osage orange, the best material for homemade bows. The Osage Indians were very feared because they had superior bow material. The Osage nation (or "People of the Middle Waters") developed in the Ohio valley around 700 BC. In the seventeenth century, the Iroquois tribe invaded the Ohio valley looking for new hunting grounds and drove the Osage tribes west into Missouri.

Native Americans used to come to Missouri to trade for the Osage-orange bows. These bows were so prized for their resilient nature that they were found over two thousand miles away in other tribes, often sought after and distributed through trade. I need to go to the Osage orange grove. Take my backpack, a ziplock bag, the big knife, and string for the bow. Put the leaf in the door, and head down to the pasture. There are plenty of wild turkeys around here. Hear that gobbling sound? That's turkey! It is not turkey season, but no one cares out here. No stops along the way.

I am at Horse's pasture. Let me grab the flour sack of acorn meats from the spring, put it in a ziplock bag and into my backpack.

Here's a good-size piece of Osage orange, just a little taller than me. My hand fits around it nicely in the middle. It is dry and dead but not gray and cracking. No knots. No twists. It is thicker at the center. It will make a good bow. With my knife, I'll shave a taper at both ends. Cut notches a couple of inches in from the ends to tie the string. The string needs to be slightly shorter than the bow. Tie one end, flex the bow, and slip the knot over the other end and tighten. Now hang it upside down by the bow middle from that strong branch over there. Pull slowly down on the string. Keep shaving the middle of the bow until it pulls down the distance from my jaw to my fully extended arm. Good. This will do.

Now for some straight, dry, and dead Osage orange sticks about half the length of the bow. Cut a small notch on the back end of each arrow to fit on the string. Just whittle the tips to a point; don't need arrowheads. This is really primitive but should work. Let's try it out on that mound of dirt over there. Pretty good. Try again with the bow sideways. It's actually more accurate than I thought it would be. Collect the arrows and maybe sharpen them some more. Luckily my grandparents had me frequently practicing with a bow and arrow since shooting a turkey with a bow and arrow is difficult. We're ready. Now, where's the gobbling coming from?

Here are some three-toed turkey tracks. Turkeys see in full color, have telescopic vision, and have good hearing. Their sense of smell is not one of their better senses. They can fly fifty-five miles per hour over short distances. Surprisingly, domesticated turkeys cannot fly since they have been bred for huge breasts. Turkeys roost in trees at night for protection from predators and come down at dawn. The tracks seem to head in this direction. I will try to get ahead of them and lie in wait. To surprise a turkey, you must sit on the ground. This means using the bow sideways.

There's some gobbling sounds coming. Only male turkeys gobble, and they spread their handsome tail feathers to attract a mate. Get several arrows ready. Be positive. They're almost here. Shoot. Got a male. He is somewhat dark with a bronze-green iridescence for most of his plumage, and he has beautiful colors: reds, greens, and coppers, dark wings boldly barred with white, rump and tail feathers tipped in white. The others flew off.

I can hold the dead turkey by the feet while I walk back to the cabin. Made it. I will chop off his head with the axe and hang him from the branch of a tree with string on his feet so the blood will drain. Let me start a fire in the outside firepit with cotton balls and petroleum jelly. Fill the stockpot with water, and put it on the grate to pluck the turkey feathers. I also need to start a fire in the oven to cook the turkey. It is warm, and I hate to fire up the oven, but I can't easily cook the turkey on an open fire.

I need to eat something. A salad will have to do. That will hold me. Bring the roasting pan and a ziplock bag outside. It is going to take a lot of plucking to get these beautiful feathers out since turkeys have some 3,500 feathers. Hold the turkey by the feet and dunk it into the water seven seconds at a time. Pull the feathers out in the direction they grew so it won't tear the skin. By dunking only seven seconds at a time, the bird won't start to cook. Wow. It's a lot of work plucking a turkey. Repeat the dipping and plucking. Feathers are out. Now find the breastbone and open the cavity. Plunge my hand in there and drag out all the innards. Save the heart, liver, and gizzard, and put the rest in a ziplock bag. Check that the cavity is clean and put the acorn meats and giblets in it. Now put it into the roasting pan. Take the boiling water off the fire. When the water has cooled, I can use it to clean up this mess.

Take the roasting pan inside. The turkey is around seven pounds. Use some oil all over the skin, wrap it in foil, and put it in the oven. In a few hours I should have a great meal. Wash my hands. For now, I will keep the bow and arrows on the top bunk. Signal is thumping. I need to reassure him.

"Signal is a good bunny. Don't worry, it's a turkey, not a rabbit. I am just really hungry. I better open the shutters to get some of this smell out. Signal, you are walking around. Rabbits can walk as well as hop. This is good since if you hop you have to land on your front feet, which doesn't work right now."

I need to rotate the turkey in the oven. While the turkey is cooking, I can turn on the crystal radio and see if I can find out something.

Here goes my memory again.

A crystal radio needs no external power. It uses only the power of the received radio signal to produce sound. I've got a large antenna, which is necessary. It is named for its most important component, a crystal detector. The earliest practical use was to receive Morse code signals transmitted from spark-gap transmitters by early amateur radio enthusiasts. As electronics evolved, the ability to send voice signals by radio caused a technological explosion around 1920 that evolved into today's radio broadcasting industry. Crystal radios also have the advantage that they cannot be located by GPS. Let's get the local station on the radio and hear what's going on. Crystal radios have a weak signal, so I will have to put in these earphones. It is still difficult to hear.

The University of Missouri owns their own local radio and TV stations. That's because they opened the first journalism school in the US in 1908 and have been consistently ranked in the top 5 journalism schools ever since. Founded in 1839, MU is a land-grant university and was the first public university west of the Mississippi river.

Right now they are playing music, but it's close to the hour, so the news should come on shortly.

Oh no! The Columbia Police are saying that Disk Banks, a member of the campus police force, was found dead in my apartment. There is a major investigation going on, and I am a person of interest.

Do my grandparents know I am a person of interest? I could call them, but if I use my cell phone, it could be quickly traced. This is an absolute catastrophe. I must get my memory back. I don't believe I would kill anyone.

Everything should be cooked. This is a great feast, and there will be plenty left for tomorrow. Let's keep some of these very colorful feathers. I should disperse the rest of the entrails in the creek. Let me put the ziplock bag in my backpack, along with soap and a towel so I can get the blood off horse. I can carry the water jugs in my hands. Put the leaf in the door. I am glad that I can finally walk more normally.

The walk to the creek is beautiful. There are bluebirds that are nesting in holes created in trees by woodpeckers, with their openings facing east away from prevailing winds. The males are bright blue, with orange bellies. So many melodious songs. Some of them have nesting material in their beaks. Some are passing insects to their female partners' mouths. Always busy.

The bluebird is the Missouri state bird; also New York's. I can hear a pileated woodpecker in the distance. They really do sound quite a bit like the cartoon bird Woody Woodpecker, a sort of laughing sound. There are a lot of mammal tracks along this trek to the creek. Most of them are nocturnal, so I only see evidence of them from their tracks. There are quite a few raccoon and possum tracks. Possums do not play dead as people think. They pass out from fear of their predators. I really hope I don't encounter a skunk.

Various hawks are all around in the sky, especially redtails. There is a great horned owl perched in a tree. Several scissortail flycatchers have flown by also. They are the state bird of Oklahoma.

This trail is a real wonderland. Let me throw the entrails into the creek and dispose of this ziplock bag back at the cabin. The creek is gurgling loudly today. Probably from the rain yesterday. Now back to the pasture.

"Come here, Horse. I got the towel wet in the spring. Good boy. Let me rub this soapy towel on your bloodstains. It is impossible to get it all off, but I don't want you to attract flies, ticks, or mosquitoes. That's better. Let me rub your nose and forehead. There. I'll massage under your forelock and under your mane gently. Good boy. Both rabbits and horses like to have their noses petted."

Now fill the water jugs and head back to the cabin. Oh no. There are tire tracks in the mud in front of the cabin. Someone has been here. The leaf is still in the door, so they didn't go into the cabin. Go inside, put the bar on the door, and get my bow and arrow. This is really frightening. Who was here? Were they here to kill me? I am afraid to go outside. I need a plan. If someone tries to break in, I can put the table on its side and get behind it with the bow and arrow. That is all I have for weapons except for martial arts.

To comfort myself when stressed, I like to remember things about my parents. My mother's hands were so soft and smooth, and she would let me play with her fingers. Her hair always smelled comforting. My parents and I would alternate making up parts of a story. Each of us had to continue the story from where the other left off. Dad's stories were always about sports and sports announcers. Mom's stories contained fashionable clothes in detail. My stories usually contained astronauts. My favorite alone-time play was to draw on upside-down cardboard boxes with crayons. I'd draw magical buttons and levers and have wonderful adventures in space.

My dreams were nearly always about flying, leaping into the air, and doing the breaststroke. Any dangers in dreams could be escaped by flying away. Landing consisted of treading air like water to land gently. Flying was always great fun. Once I had a horrible nightmare that I was tied with a logging chain around one ankle in a room with no windows. Dad calmed me down with one of his many stories he'd make up just for me. My parents were so much fun to be with. Lots of laughter, games, and lessons. It seemed like the end of the world when my grandparents told me my parents had been killed when I was seven years old. I miss my parents very much.

"Signal, I think I have had enough of this day. I will give you some more food and go to bed. Let me lock the shutters and door. I will keep the bow and arrows in bed with me. Feels good to lie down and close my eyes, but I doubt I will sleep very well. It took all day yesterday to catch and cook a catfish for protein. Today it took all day to catch and cook a turkey. Looks like it is going to be a full-time job just to get food out here."

5

Hunting Memory

I just woke up. Terrible night's sleep. Everything in these bizarre circumstances is becoming overwhelming. Is this my life now? What if it is? Every day was so structured before: gym, university, trash day, etc. Just busy every minute of the day with routines, research, and teaching. Now what? And I am worried about those tire tracks I saw yesterday.

"Signal, how are you doing? Where are you? Are you making me search for you? I can't see you. You must be under the bed. Later I'll move the saddlebags to the upper bunk so you can't chew on them. I guess you are getting around much better. We need to get you some more greens today, but getting out of bed seems monumental. Let me just roll over and sleep some more."

My life seems so strange now. Well, it's not as bad as Camus's Sisyphus who had to push a boulder up a mountain every day just to have it roll back down and start over the next day. It's not as bad as Kafka's *Metamorphosis*, where the character wakes up as a huge insect one day. Or is it? My whole life has been routines and working toward goals. Now what?

I need to get up and get going. I will start a fire in the stove and put a kettle of water on for coffee and oatmeal. Just throw in some wood and put a kettle of water on the stove. I still have some greens for Signal. They stay fresh in a mug of water. Fill his water bowl. I will do my morning routine. It will be nice having a hot meal.

While the water is heating, let me make turkey soup. I can take the turkey meat off the bones and put them in the stockpot. I have dried vegetables, rice, and spices. Add water and put it on the stove. Now I'll have my coffee and oatmeal.

I can check the radio to see what is going on with my case. I wish I could remember what happened. I can't make a plan until I have the facts at my disposal. The police are still looking for Coral Holmes as a person of interest in the death of the university police officer Disk Banks, who was found dead in my apartment. The medical examiner reports that the officer died from blunt force trauma to the head. They also found a pistol with a silencer in the wastebasket in the kitchen with my fingerprints on it. There was blood all over the apartment. Disk had gunshot residue on his hand, but he did not have any bloody wounds. So they assume I was the one shot. I don't remember any of this.

I desperately need to get my short-term memory back. It should return over time by itself as long as there is no long-term brain damage. I will throw the turkey bones behind the cabin for animals to eat.

Oh no! I hear an all-terrain vehicle coming. I could be in serious danger. Let me run inside and get my bow and arrows. I see a guy on an ATV wearing an orange vest and carrying a rifle. This is very disconcerting. My heart is racing. I can hold the bow and arrows like I am going out target shooting so it doesn't look threatening. Step outside.

"What are you doing here?"

"I own the ranch on the west side of this property. My name is Hunter."

I have no idea if he is legit, so I can't turn my back on him.

"So you left the $10 bill and a note by the whiskey bottle."

"Yes, last fall I took shelter in the log cabin."

"My grandparents call me Memory. This is their log cabin. There is actually a Log Cabin Day. In 1989, the Michigan legislature passed a resolution making the last Sunday in June Log Cabin Day. Also the famous architect Frank Lloyd Wright designed the Imperial Hotel in Tokyo to make it earthquake-proof. It had interlocking log beams. It was one of the few buildings to survive the 1923 Great

Kanto Earthquake that destroyed Tokyo. This design inspired his son John Lloyd Wright to invent Lincoln Logs in 1924. Wright named the toy after President Abraham Lincoln, who was born in a log cabin in Illinois in 1809. So what are you doing here?"

"I raise sheep, and the coyotes have been killing them. I asked your grandfather if I could hunt them on his land, and he said it was fine. He said he had his wife and granddaughter here with him."

"Hunter, most people don't know that roquefort cheese is sheep cheese. It is aged in caves in the town of Roquefort-sur-Soulzon in southern France."

"I certainly did not know that, Memory."

"Hunter, llamas can be used as guards against coyote attacks on sheep herds. Just one guard llama is an effective protector of a small herd and can even kill an attacking coyote."

"Why did they not teach me that in AG school? Thank you so much for that information."

I don't like this. I don't know him, and I am still skeptical. "Then why have I never met you, Hunter?"

"Your grandfather told me to hunt away from the cabin so no one was in danger. So I never met you. I saw the smoke from your cabin yesterday and decided to check it out, since your grandparents have not been here in quite a while. But no one was here."

"I saw your tire tracks. You use a rifle to hunt coyote?"

"Your grandfather said no traps, so I use a rifle. The semiautomatic MSR-15 Long Range is the best coyote gun. Its high muzzle velocity and flat trajectory will take out a coyote at four hundred yards. FMJ ammunition will preserve the hide. These hides sell for up to $100 on the open market."

"So you are a hunter, and your name is Hunter. Are you pulling my leg? How often do you hunt?"

"Yes, my name really is Hunter, and I hunt every day now."

"So you are a sheep rancher."

"Yes. I went through the Division of Animal Sciences in the College of Agriculture, Food, and Natural Resources program at the University of Missouri. This is a world-class department with two National Academy of Sciences members and three National Academy of Inventors members. They are ranked as one of the top-ten animal science programs in the nation. In 2020, they celebrated one hundred fifty years of serving the state of Missouri. After I graduated, I got an MBA so I could run my parents' ranch. I took over the ranch three years ago and converted it from raising cattle to raising sheep. The ranch is two thousand acres. We currently have one thousand acres of wheat and five thousand sheep. My parents then moved to St. Louis and live near the St. Louis Gateway Arch."

"Hunter, the St. Louis Arch is a weighted catenary, which is the Latin word for 'chain.' If you hang a chain by its ends, it forms the shape of the arch. This design is the most efficient way to equalize the pressure of the arch, since all the weight on the top is pushing directly down the legs and pinning them to the ground."

"How do you know that?"

"I have an eidetic memory and read a lot. An eidetic memory is sometimes called a 'photographic memory.' Why did you switch from raising cattle to raising sheep?"

"There are many advantages to raising sheep. To move an obstinate cow, I have to go back to the ranch and saddle a horse. With a sheep, I can just grab them up and carry them where they belong. Also, you do not have to worry about getting squashed by sheep. Twenty people a year are killed in the US by cows. Other advantages are that sheep eat weeds that cattle won't graze on so I can use them to control weeds on the harvested wheat fields. There are also financial benefits. A cow can bring in $500 at auction. A ninety-pound sheep will bring in $100, and a female sheep will have three lambs a year. Since I replaced each cow with six sheep, the added profit is immense. They eat about the same. But if you lose a cow, you lose $500, and if you lose a sheep, you just lose $100. The complex part is fencing since it is difficult to hold sheep in, but I eventually changed the cow fences into sheep fences. My father is deaf, so the ranch is called the Silent Ranch and our brand is DEAF. I am a CODA—child of deaf adult."

"So you know sign language."

"Yes."

"Hunter, sign language is the third most-studied language in the US, and two out of every one thousand babies in the US are born deaf. I also went to the University of Missouri and had majors in computer engineering, mathematics, and psychology."

Wish I had not said that. That information may come out on the news, and it is critical he not know who I am. Since my name is different from my grandfather's, he should not know my real name. This guy seems like he may be legit, but I still have to be careful. He seems very easy to talk to, but I need to stay on guard and not reveal anything else about myself.

"Memory, what do you do for a living?"

I can't tell him that I work at the University of Missouri, or he will know who I am. I need something fast.

"I work for a hedge fund in Boston."

"Any fund I would know?"

"No, it is a small private fund."

"Then what are you doing here?"

"I am visiting my grandparents for a month."

"Why are they not here?"

"They are too old to make the trip here any longer."

"Why aren't you with them?"

This guy is awfully inquisitive. It worries me. He seems to want to know a lot about me.

"I used to spend summers here with my grandparents and was dying to see the place again."

"Memory, if you work for a hedge fund, you must be computer literate. I took some computer courses so I can keep the records for the ranch: buy everything I need online, keep track of taxes, and more. Also, I use drones to keep track of the sheep. I actually graduated from the Agriculture Systems Technology program. This program provides links among the researcher, designer, engineer, manufacturer, and the consumer. I also do sheep research for the university."

"Hunter, I know the university has a famous agriculture department. Ernie Sears worked there for years. He was an American geneticist, botanist, pioneer of plant genetics, and the leading expert on wheat cytogenetics. He won the Wolf Prize in Israel. It is considered the most prestigious prize in agriculture."

"Memory, it was awarded to Sears because he developed a type of wheat which grows in arid soil and is now feeding millions of hungry people on earth. Funny you should mention that. Sears was my advisor's advisor, so I heard a lot about him. I need to get back to my ranch. I will come by again tomorrow. Do you need anything?"

"You are a real cowboy with jeans, cowboy hat and boots, and a pullover shirt under your orange vest for the hot summer. Do you have another cowboy hat? I could use one since I am outside a lot. I could also use some eggs, bread, Bisquick, maple syrup, a jar of raspberry jam, and a large jar of crunchy peanut butter. I have money. Tomorrow I will give you a shopping list. Bye, Hunter."

"Let me write this down. How did you end up here without the basic food groups?"

"I decided to challenge myself and rough it. Why are you so inquisitive, Hunter?"

"You are the most interesting person I have met in a very long time. I was hoping to get to know you. I don't mean it to be prying. I need to go. I'll see you tomorrow."

I need to give the cabin a careful cleaning. I can sweep the floor with the broom and get up the dirt with the dustpan. Now I need to clean up the shelves, the stove area, and the basin area. Next, I need to clean up Signal's area. This was time-consuming but worth it.

Let me give Signal some water and greens. I have turkey soup for lunch. I love all the vegetables, spices, and turkey. Glad I made it. I am still a little tired every day and have no memory of how I got here. This is a disaster.

"Signal, I just met the most interesting guy. He looks exactly my size and is a handsome cowboy. He got me out of my funk, and he is coming back tomorrow. At least I have something to look forward to. But I don't know him, so I may be in danger. I will have to be very careful since he carries a gun. Also, he asks a lot of questions. He may not be what he seems. I need to stay on guard and not reveal anything else about myself.

"I better check the news again. The police report they found dozens of martial arts trophies and books in my apartment. Since Disk Banks died of a broken neck, I am a person of interest in his murder. They have sent out a BOLO for me and are looking for my car."

This day has been overwhelming, and there is still a lot left to it. I will not go outside again today. It's so quiet in the cabin, and the hopelessness of my circumstance has caused my memories to have their way with me—every embarrassing moment, every joy, every tragedy, every insignificant event I have ever been through. I've got to stop this bombardment. I took piano lessons from age five to age twelve. So let me use some notepad pages cut lengthwise and taped end to end with duct tape. Draw all eighty-eight keys of a piano keyboard, both black and white keys. Since I remember the piano pieces I've played and know how they sound, I can imagine hearing what I'm playing.

The duct tape bleeds through a little, but it's okay. Put the paper keyboard on the table and play.

It's working! I'll keep playing these pieces to relax my mind. Keep track of time. Let's see how long I need to play until I get control over these bothersome memories. Then I'll be able to think clearly again in the present. Maybe I will take a short nap. Lie on the bunk bed and close my eyes.

That felt really good. I can play my piano again. That used up the afternoon. I need to put these papers on the shelf so they don't get dirty. Signal didn't complain since this is a silent piano. There are so many things that need to be figured out. But they will have to wait for tomorrow.

I will finish the leftover turkey soup for dinner. Let me heat it on the stove. I can feed Signal in the meantime. Another great meal. I'm very tired.

"Signal, we need to go to sleep since Hunter is coming again tomorrow. The bar is on the door. Go in your house where you are safe, and I will take the bottom bunk as usual. Wow! I have a usual in this unusual situation."

6

Wooden Canoe People

A good night's sleep, but I can't stay here forever. I need to get my memory back so I can get out of here. I can't believe the police think I killed someone. This is not possible.

"Signal, I'm up. Here's your breakfast. For me, it is coffee and oatmeal again. While the kettle heats on the stove, I can do my routine: wash up, brush teeth, comb hair, clean wounds, and then eat. Hunter is bringing me stuff today. I hope I can get Hunter to regularly supply us with food. I do have plenty of money in my wallet. I already hear the ATV coming. I better carry the bow and arrow again."

"Hi, Hunter. I have never seen such a large ATV."

"This is a 6×6 Outlander. It has six tires and a small bed like a truck so we can carry things around the ranch. I brought the things you requested. I threw in some sheep butter, a bag of oranges, and some sandwiches you can have for lunch. There is roast beef and ham."

"Hunter, let me put the food in the cabin and come back. How much do I owe you?"

"We can settle up another day. I ordered four llamas yesterday when I got home. They should arrive within a week. Thank you for telling me about this. Maybe I'll stop losing sheep. Why are you carrying a bow and arrow and have a turkey feather in your hair?"

"I killed a turkey the other day and was trying to look presentable."

"You killed a turkey with a bow and arrow?"

"Yes, I did."

"Very impressive. Turkey are not easy to hunt even with a rifle."

"Hunter, you can follow their three-toed tracks in the dirt. To hunt them with a bow, you must sit on the ground quietly so they do not see you. Room is at a premium for drawing back the bow."

"Memory, gobblers living out in the wild are some of the smartest and wariest creatures in the woods. Hunting them requires a mastery of turkey language and a solid understanding of stealth and camouflage. I can't believe you actually caught one with a bow. Are you short of food?"

"Yes, I am short of food. Here is a shopping list."

"Memory, do you need a gun?"

"No, thank you. I know nothing about guns. I also caught a catfish by hand."

"You're quite the survivalist, Memory. Perhaps I have things to learn from you. For the fun of it, I watched *The Wizard of Oz* last night."

"It is a wonderful movie. I saw it as a child. But there are several inaccuracies in the movie. First, the Tin Man would not rust since tin is resistant to rust. In fact, the inside of a steel food can has a tin covering to keep it from rusting. Second, after the scarecrow gets his diploma in 'Thinkology,' he immediately incorrectly states the Pythagorean theorem. He says, 'The sum of the square roots of any two sides of an isosceles triangle is equal to the square root of the third side.' Putting in the square root is wrong, and the statement is for right triangles. The Pythagorean theorem actually states the sum of the squares of the sides of a right triangle equals the square of the hypotenuse.

"For example, 3, 4, 5 forms a right triangle since $3^2 + 4^2 = 9 + 16 = 25 = 5^2$."

"Memory, you really are a wealth of information."

"Hunter, I have a swamp rabbit in the cabin. His name is Signal. A coyote attacked him and broke his leg. Do you want to see him?"

"For sure."

"Come into the cabin."

"You have a stove, Memory."

"Yes, and it is complicated to cook on. It has two fireboxes on the left. The top one just heats the burners, and the other heats the oven. You control the heat by opening a vent which determines how much air is fed to the fire. There is a sliding mechanism which diverts the heat to go around the oven box before it escapes to the flue. This heats the oven more consistently. The oven is hotter towards the firebox, so you need to rotate the food halfway through cooking. The surface has three temperature zones, with the hottest right next to the firebox. You have to be careful what you put on the stove since the surface is cast iron and will rust. It is a skill to know how much wood is needed for each function."

"Hi, Signal. I'm Hunter. I hear you have had a rough time. Signal just ran into his house."

"He is not used to strangers. He will warm up to you quickly. He did to me. Just don't sing to him."

"Memory, a group of rabbits is called a fluffle, and a baby rabbit is called a kit. The female is a doe, and the male is a buck. Signal has poops on his moss. Rabbits are one of few animals who poop where they eat. Rabbits are herbivores that feed by grazing on grass and other leafy plants. As a consequence, their diet contains large amounts of cellulose, which is hard to digest. Rabbits solve this problem by a form of hindgut fermentation. They pass two distinct types of feces: soft black viscous pellets and then hard droppings. Rabbits re-ingest their first droppings to digest their food further and extract sufficient nutrients. So when you see a rabbit with its head between its legs, it is not licking himself like a dog, but rather it's eating what we call 'power poops.'"

"How do you know that?"

"I did get a degree in animal science, and I graduated at the top of my class."

"So we both grew up in Missouri and went to the University of Missouri. Missouri was named after a tribe of Sioux Indians called the Missouris. While often mistranslated as 'muddy water,' the word actually means 'town of the large canoes' or 'wooden canoe people.' Europeans arrived in Missouri in the late 1600s. This area became known as the Missouri Territory, so when it became a state, it adopted the name Missouri."

"Very few people know that, Memory."

"My eidetic memory again. I can't help it or control it as well as I'd like."

"Memory, Signal just came out. He has been chewing his duct tape. Tomorrow I will bring him a leg brace that he can't chew off."

"Hunter, he is also chewing on the table legs. Please bring me something to put on the table, chair, and bed legs to prevent the gnawing."

"I see on the shelf two sheets of paper with identical lists. Why do you have two identical lists?"

"I hit my head and was checking to see if I have amnesia."

"Is this like in the movie *50 First Dates*? When I come back tomorrow you may not know who I am?"

"Do you care?"

"I was hoping not to be grilled again about what I am doing here."

"Are you afraid you'll forget your story?"

"It won't matter what story I tell if you can't remember."

"Point taken."

"So when I return tomorrow, I will have to make you fall in love with me all over again."

"Are you crazy, Hunter? I am not in love with you now."

"Maybe you just forgot."

"Hunter, I have an eidetic memory."

"That's okay. I can wait for you to fall in love with me."

"Hunter, I have only met you twice. Isn't this a little overboard? You are scaring me."

"I apologize for scaring you. I was just bantering to see how you would react. You will learn that I love to banter. I love the challenge."

"Hunter, the main types of bantering are witty flirting, mild sarcasm, self-deprecating humor, playful teasing, and goofy responses."

"I do all of the above, Memory."

"I used to come here often with my grandparents but have not been here since I went to graduate school eight years ago. I needed a vacation. I didn't realize how difficult it is to get food out here."

"I see a horse in the pasture, but you do not have a saddle and bridle in here. Why did you come without a saddle and bridle on the horse?"

He is probing for information again. This makes me nervous. "Sorry, but without my short-term memory, I don't know."

"I need to go. I will see you tomorrow. Good to see you again."

"Good to know you too, Hunter."

It is time for lunch. I will have sandwiches and oranges. These are delicious. I need to clean the ashes out of the stove. There is a scoop on the shelf, and I can put the ashes in the stockpot and take them to the outhouse. Again, be careful when opening the door in case some animal has made it inside. I'll dump the ashes into the hole to help keep the smell down. Back to the cabin.

I need to listen to the radio. Dr. Ed Green of UC Santa Cruz developed a method to extract DNA from hair, which does not have roots. So they used my hairbrush to discover that the blood in the apartment was mine. They are contacting all hospitals within one hundred miles to see if I showed up.

"Signal, I will try to work on my research this afternoon to get my mind off my situation. I can put my notes on the table and use a notepad. I have two major research projects right now. One is a joint grant with Agriculture and the Medical School. I don't have what I need to do this research here. The other concerns artificial intelligence. I seem to have brought some of my notes on this in the saddlebags."

Unfortunately, I am having trouble concentrating, but I will still try. Not much progress. I should go to the outhouse and bring in some firewood on the way back.

Back to research. Still no progress, but at least that used up the afternoon.

I have some new food. I will have a sandwich, an orange, and some water for dinner.

"MEMORY" SURVIVAL

"Signal, it is late. We need to go to sleep before it gets dark so I don't have to use the headlamp or candles. Here's some greens and water. See you in the morning. I will secure the door and shutters and go to bed."

I just jerked awake. I was having a nightmare that someone was trying to break in. Wait! Signal is thumping and thumping. Maybe someone *is* trying to get in here. It is very difficult to get through the barn door locks, but if someone is here to kill me, they could shoot their way through the door. I may not have a chance to use martial arts since they may know that Disk Banks was killed that way and will be on guard.

Signal is still thumping. My heart is pounding. I'm sweating. I need a quick plan for a worst-case scenario. Let me turn the table on its side and get behind it with my bow and arrow. I can't be directly in front of the door in case someone shoots through it. I will slide the table over next to the shelves. I don't have any other weapons, but I can put the carving knife and my grandfather's walking stick next to me. As a last-ditch effort, I can throw books. I am not going down without a fight to the end.

Signal has stopped thumping, but I am not sure what that means. Someone could still be outside. I will have to wait until I think it is safe. Stay behind the table in the meantime. I will put on my headlamp, hold the bow and arrow, and open a shutter a crack. Now I see what happened. There are coyote tracks in front of the cabin. I was lucky this time.

"Thanks for alerting me, Signal. I am going to have trouble relaxing and going back to sleep, but eventually, I hope to make it. I will lie in bed, take deep breaths over and over, and tense and relax various muscle groups. Ah. That's better. Good night, Signal."

7

A Walking Encyclopedia

I overslept, and someone is pounding on the door. My heart is racing again. Grab the bow and arrow. Oh, I hear Hunter calling my name. Hunter was acting a little strange yesterday. All the more reason to be wary of him. He seems nice enough, but I better stay on guard. I will take the bar off the door and open it.

"Who are you?"

"Oh no, Memory. You lost your memory."

"Sorry, Hunter, I couldn't resist. My memory is fine. Come on in."

"Memory, are we rearranging the furniture? Why is the table on its side?"

"I had a terrible night. Signal wouldn't stop thumping, so I thought someone was trying to break in. I got behind the table with my bow and arrow. My heart was pounding. I have never been so terrified. As it turns out, it was just a pack of coyotes in front of the cabin."

"You said you did not want a gun, so tomorrow I will bring you two cans of hornet spray. I don't use mace for protection since it has a short range and a determined individual can overcome it. But hornet spray shoots twenty feet and is a deadly poison, so if they don't back off, it's a trip to the hospital. It is actually illegal to use hornet spray on a human. But if someone is trying to kill you, all bets are off.

You should carry it at all times since there are dangerous animals all around here. Do you have a cell phone?"

This is tricky. I can't tell him I have a cell phone but keep it in a Faraday bag so it can't be traced, or that will set off red flags.

"No."

"Why would you come here without a cell phone?"

He is probing again. I really need to be careful. "As I said, I decided to rough it."

"I will also buy two burner phones so we can talk. Since you will be using it infrequently, the battery should last at least a week. Then I can swap them out and take one with me to charge it. I brought the stuff you wanted: toilet paper, paper towels, Kleenex, a box of fire starters, a canned ham, canned beans, spaghetti and sauce, some timothy hay pellets for Signal, sour apple spray to deter Signal from chewing wood, Cheerios, a sketch pad and drawing pencils, music score paper with lines for the notes, and some carrots for Signal and the horse."

"For your information, the horse's name is Horse."

"That's original. I also brought a can opener, a leg brace for Signal, a ball for Signal to push around, and a cooler filled with ice so you can store food. In it I put cheddar cheese, sliced beef and ham, mayonnaise, milk, and potato salad. When I came inside yesterday to see Signal, I noticed that it is quite hot in here. So I brought a portable fan with two boxes of twenty-four batteries each. And so you do not have to make a fire inside, I brought you a gas grill. It is a three-burner grill with front doors, and I put an extra tank of gas inside. Help me put it out front of the cabin. Let me upright the table and put the cooler under it. This should stay cold for five days. It will take two of us to bring in all the rest. You can pay me another time."

"Thank you. I have a can opener on my Swiss army knife, but it is difficult to use. What is this brace, Hunter?"

"We use them on rabbits when needed. You pick up Signal and hold him on the sides with his legs pointed at me. I brought heavy elbow-length leather gloves we use working with animals. This is so his hind feet toenails don't tear a gash in my arm. He is squirming and kicking. I got his duct tape off. Oh, he does not have a broken leg, it's only sprained, so he should be fine within a week. I just have to put on the brace and tighten it."

"That was thoughtful of you. Thank you. I missed breakfast and taking care of Signal. Let me feed Signal."

"I brought lamb burger, buns, onions, and some tomatoes. Lamb burger is ten times more flavorful than hamburger. We can put onion and tomatoes on the burgers, and you will have some left over for later. Since you haven't eaten, we can make the burgers right now."

"Okay. Let me start my new gas grill, put on a kettle of water for coffee, and the lamb burgers. I'll be right back."

"You need to turn on the gas at the tank. The grill has a spark starter. Signal, here are some timothy hay pellets and carrots for you. These are your favorites. Rabbit's ears are made for an excellent sense of hearing which helps protect them from predators. You have something in common with Horse. You both have your eyes on the side of your head. This has the advantage that you have almost 360-degree vision, but it has the disadvantage that you cannot see directly in front of your face. That is why when you stand up on your hind legs you put your front paws down at your sides since you cannot use them to eat like squirrels do.

"When you put your face in a bowl of food, people think you are looking at the food. Actually, you cannot see the food. You use your excellent sense of smell to detect what and where the food is. Twitching your nose stimulates millions of scent receptors and improves the number of scents you can distinguish in a short period of time. Like many other rabbit features, this has played an important role in a wild rabbit's survival. Rabbits can twitch their noses up to 120 times per minute. This gives them the ability to sense dangerous predators who are out of sight."

"Hunter. You really do know stuff."

"There goes my degree in animal sciences again."

"Hunter, let's go outside."

"Memory, I can see from here that the pasture is fenced with Osage orange trees. These trees grow very rapidly."

"Yes, but one of the fastest-growing plants on the planet is bamboo. It can grow an incredible three feet in a day."

"Information just dribbles out of you, Memory."

"There is sliced tomato and onion on the table. The lamb burgers are done, so we can bring them and the kettle inside. This is delicious, Hunter. Wish I'd discovered it earlier. Hunter, do you have books on sign language?"

"Yes, I'll bring some tomorrow."

"I am still having trouble concentrating from my head injury."

"Memory, can I help you with your concentration in some way?"

"I don't know what you could do."

"Let's try remembering a word list. I made one for you last night. I used to play this game with my parents."

"I have an eidetic memory, so if I see a list, I will remember it. Let's try it, and I can show you how to win this game."

"I will read you the list: *lion, window, sausage, table, racket, computer, bottle, ink, pencil, teacher, prison, sand, hair, banana, toast.* Later you will give it back to me."

"Hunter, Signal is rubbing his chin on everything."

"Rabbits have scent glands under their chins. They rub their chins on things that they want to claim as theirs. You are lucky you do not have a line of poops down the middle of the cabin. Rabbits make a line of poops to establish territory. Other rabbits will not cross the line. Signal is really attacking the carrots I brought him. Signal, this will build up your strength. You are going to have a great sex life. Female rabbits usually have four litters annually. Each litter contains an average of five babies, and female rabbits can get pregnant again almost immediately after giving birth. Since they are prey, they need to reproduce a lot."

"Hunter, did you actually have to bring up sex?"

"Is this a forbidden subject?"

"No, but I went to college at age twelve. Before I left, my grandmother handed me a stack of books on sex and birth control. At twelve this was disgusting. It was how I imagined physical assault. When I got to college, it seemed like that was all anyone ever talked about. I think they did it partly to make me uncomfortable. I wanted nothing to do with it. I was not on birth control, and if I got pregnant, my grandiose future plans would have been in jeopardy, and I never understood the connection between dating and sex. So I did not date."

"So you are a virgin, and a brilliant one at that."

"I like being a virgin. I would have preferred not going here, but since we have, what about your sex life?"

"I was awkward around females. I also was afraid of getting someone pregnant and ruining my future. So I also didn't really date in college."

"So you are one of the few adult male virgins in the US."

"I stared at a pretty girl once. Does that count?"

"Depends. Did you have a climax?"

"No. That's not appropriate in front of the library. Have you had a climax?"

"I wouldn't know."

"How is it that you never got married? You are so beautiful. The guys should be all over you."

"Yes, but guys are attracted to looks. I want someone who likes me for my brain."

"You have a very attractive brain, Memory."

"Did you just turn my brain into a sensual object? I am not sure how to respond to that."

"Do you want to learn about sex?"

"You don't know anything about sex, Hunter."

"So we can learn together."

"Who said I want to learn?"

"Everyone wants to learn."

"You are getting weird again, Hunter. Should I be scared?"

"Sorry, Memory. I just can't help bantering, it comes naturally to me. And you are especially cute when frustrated."

"Bantering is new to me. I will take 'being cute' as a compliment although that is not a given."

"Memory, now give me back my list."

"*Lion, window, sausage, table, racket, computer, bottle, ink, pencil, teacher, prison, sand, hair, banana, toast.*"

"How did you do that? You even got the words in order."

"To remember a word list, you make a story that is easy to remember and contains the words. For this I composed in my head 'A mountain lion came in the window after the sausage on the table, and I chased it away with a racket. The computer is down, and the bottle of ink spilled, so I had to use a pencil. I feel like I'm a teacher in a prison with sand in my hair and no banana, just this piece of toast.'

"By the way, Hunter, humans share 50 percent of their DNA with bananas. All living things on earth share some DNA. That is because we all evolved from a common ancestor, a single-celled organism from four billion years ago called the 'last universal common ancestor' (LUCA). National Banana Day is April 17th."

"That is impressive, Memory. It is fun coming here."

"I enjoy your company also."

"We may have to stop meeting this way, or people are going to talk."

"Hunter, they have been talking about me my whole life."

"Why?"

"That will have to wait for a future time."

"I'll see you tomorrow, Memory. I'll come early since four months ago a car in front of me jumped a red light, caused an accident, and I have to testify in court tomorrow afternoon."

"Hunter, today the word *testify* generally means 'witness.' But it can also mean 'testicle.' *Testify* comes from the Latin word *testis*, which means both 'witness' and 'testicles.' This goes back to ancient Rome when men would swear on their testicles to tell the truth. Thus the origin of the word *testify*. So did the word derive since they were 'bearing witness,' or did it derive because they were 'holding their testicles'? Or were these the same thing? Otherwise, why would the word have such diverse meanings?"

"That is amazing. Do you know more of these?"

"An unlimited number. Another interesting example is *infantry*. Typically in ancient times an army's infantry consisted of soldiers too young or too inexperienced to ride a horse and be part of the cavalry so they were on foot—that is, the foot soldiers were the 'infants corps,' which eventually became the word *infantry*."

"Incredible. I'm afraid I have to go. I have to vaccinate the sheep today. The most important vaccines given routinely to sheep and lambs are those used to protect against clostridial diseases."

"Hunter, the word *vaccine* means 'cow.' In the 1700s, English doctor Edward Jenner got an idea when observing milkmaids who had gotten cowpox, which is a mild virus. These people seemed to be immune to the deadly smallpox virus, which was killing millions of people. He developed a process of introducing a small amount of cowpox into people to protect them against smallpox. He called this process *vaccination* from the Latin 'vaccinus,' from *vacca*, which is 'cow.'"

"Memory, you're just a walking encyclopedia."

"Bye, Hunter. Here is a list of some more items I'd like."

I need to check the news on the radio. The police now report that they found my car in the Missouri river with blood on the seat, and the windshield was cracked with my hair stuck in the cracks. So they think I was knocked out and drowned in the river. They have brought in boats and divers and have groups searching the banks.

This is probably good news for me, but how did my car get in the river? They also sent my laptop to the FBI to see if they can break the password. They won't be able to since I have a 32-symbol password.

I wish I could remember what happened. This is disastrous. I still can't contact anyone since I don't know if I am in danger and from whom.

Hunter is a very caring person. He almost seems too good to be true. I think I'll spend the rest of the afternoon with the sketch pad and drawing pencils. This will help get my mind off this catastrophe. I can sketch some of the days since I arrived.

It takes over an hour for a good sketch. Four sketches used up the afternoon and evening. Hunter brought me sandwiches for dinner. That was nourishing. I have had enough of this day.

"Signal. It's time for bed. Here are your night treats. See you in the morning."

8

Disk Shot

I seem to have gotten a small portion of my lost memory back. I think it's from listening to what the police are saying on the radio. It's not good, but I cannot worry about it right now.

"I'm up, Signal. You drove me crazy last night pushing the ball all around the cabin. Here is some water, and you have pellets for now. I must change clothes. I'll have to put my bloody clothes back on which are washed, but I couldn't get the blood out. I'll go down to the spring to wash up and get water. Put soap and a towel in my backpack and carry the water jugs in my hands."

It's a little cool this morning. Put the leaf in the door, and head to the spring.

"Hi, Horse. Here's some carrots. Look the other way while I wash up."

This water is very cold. A soap scrubbing is a good start. I'll collect some more of this watercress. Just pinch a little off each plant so I don't kill them and put them in my backpack. Fill the water jugs. On the way back to the cabin grab some more dandelion greens, and here's some lambsquarters.

"Signal, here's your greens. I'll put a kettle of water and a skillet of eggs on the grill. I can toast the bread on the grill. I have butter. I will cook outside but eat in here with you. Signal, what are you doing between my legs? Don't you know that the most common household injury is tripping over pets? I am going to scoot you back to your area with my foot."

Let me finish making breakfast and bring it inside. This is a great breakfast. Seems almost like normal, for a change.

"I hear Hunter's ATV. Signal, you are an interesting roommate, but it is very nice having another human to talk to. I guess I am going to have to learn to like his bantering. Still, I have to be extremely careful not to reveal anything about myself. Hunter is quite smart and will figure out who I am if I give up too much information. Wait a second. Hunter says he is hunting coyotes, but I have never heard a gunshot. He may be a lousy hunter, or he may not be what he seems. I don't even know if his name is really Hunter. It could have been a spur-of-the-moment lie since he said he had been hunting. I'd better stay on guard."

Hunter is already here. It is overcast today, but it doesn't necessarily mean rain. I still worry a little if there is something going on with him. He seems too good to be true. He seems nice enough, but I need to stay alert. There still may something wrong here. Let me go outside.

"Hunter, thank you for the gas grill. What's on the back of your ATV?"

"It's a picnic table. I brought it so we can eat outside. Help me carry the table over next to the grill. I also brought the two cans of hornet spray and two burner phones. Here's my business card with both cell phone numbers on the back."

"Did you make this picnic table?"

"Yes, a year ago I made it for the ranch."

"How did you get all the parts right?"

"You use the carpenters' rule: 'Measure twice and cut once.' Memory, why are your clothes covered in dried blood?"

"As I told you, I hit my head on a rock and got quite a bloody gash. I am glad you are coming. It is nice to have someone interesting to talk to. Do you look forward to coming here?"

"It makes my day. Talking to sheep is not exactly a challenge. Before you, all I had to look forward to was going to bed at night."

"Does this make us friends, Hunter?"

"I don't know. I've never had a true friend."

"Me either, Hunter. My approach to life was not necessarily to make friends but to not make enemies. Because the secret to long-term survival is to understand that friends come and go but enemies accumulate."

"I also brought some oil, balsamic vinegar, and some sheep's cheese."

Wait a second. There is no way he could know that this is my favorite salad dressing and cheese. There is something wrong here.

"You could not know that these are my favorites, and you never shoot your gun. Who are you really? You are not just a stranger neighbor. What are you doing here?"

"You might as well know. From the moment I came here, I knew who you were. Your grandfather told me that your parents' names were Holmes and that he called you Memory. I heard on the radio that Coral Holmes was a person of interest in the apparent murder of a campus cop. When I saw the smoke from your fire, I came and pretended to be coyote hunting. I didn't shoot my gun since I didn't want to scare you."

"Why did you not tell me earlier who you were?"

"You weren't telling me the truth about yourself, so I thought it would be better if we got to know each other before I revealed myself. Also, I wanted to be sure you were all right before I called your grandfather to tell him you are okay. We became quite close over the years, and he gave me his phone number. I contacted him when I first saw you were here, and we've been in touch ever since. I talk to him on my home phone. He was very happy to hear that you are alive. He then sent me money to buy stuff for you. He made it clear that you could not have killed someone. I didn't turn you in because I trust his judgment. You should not call them on the phone since their phone may be tapped. Your grandfather and I talk in code. You are a baby lamb of his I'm keeping. So when I tell him his baby lamb is doing quite well, he understands."

"So what do you hear on the news?"

"I watched the news on TV last night, and they had a segment just on you. The police say that in your apartment they found dozens of martial arts trophies and books. Since Disk died of a broken neck, this makes you a person of interest. They found your car in the Missouri river and are searching there for you. What really happened?"

"I'm not completely sure. Apparently when I arrived here I fell off Horse and hit my head. I lost my short-term memory of that day, but this morning I finally remembered a small portion of the beginning of the day.

"I was in the kitchen of my apartment making coffee and eggs for breakfast before going to school. My roommate, Dorsa, left unusually early for work. I had martial arts class that day. I love going to class. It's challenging, and the exercise feels great. The doorbell rang. When I opened the door, a campus policeman named Disk Banks came in and closed the door. He then pulled out a gun. I could see that it had a silencer, which is legal in Missouri, but it was clearly not his service revolver.

"He said, 'I am sorry, but you cannot leave here alive.' I said, 'I don't understand.'

"He said, 'Yes, you do. You have been investigating me. I caught you following me. I can't have this. You could destroy all of my great plans. This is too important to have you ruin it.'

"I said, 'I haven't done anything to you!' He continued pointing the gun at me.

"He said, 'Don't try to lie your way out of it. You are done here and now.'

"My years of martial arts training were about to pay off. I needed to disable him. Turning my back on him to throw him off guard, I did a spinning heel kick to the side of his head. This is the most dangerous kick in martial arts. I did not intend to kill him, but probably because I was within a second of being shot, an oversupply of adrenaline caused me to kick harder than I planned. Then his gun went off, and the bullet hit me with a through and through in the left buttock.

"I panicked. The head of campus security, Birch, partnered with him since he was on probation. Birch could be close and may also want to shoot me. I had to get out of there fast. I grabbed the saddlebags for my bike and the gun. I thought he was just knocked out and might wake up, so I threw his gun in the wastebasket in the kitchen. I regularly carry in my saddlebags a rain suit, a cloth backpack, duct tape, notepads and pens, and my research notes. I quickly threw into the saddlebags bottles of water, protein bars, oil and balsamic vinegar off the counter. I grabbed sheep cheese out of the refrigerator, and peanut butter out of the cabinet. In the bathroom I grabbed gauze. I then ran to my bedroom and grabbed Faraday bags, a change of clothes, a large travel ziplock bag of toiletries, and the thumb drive, which backs up my laptop. Then I programmed the laptop to erase itself, which was not really necessary since I have a 32-symbol password, which is essentially unbreakable. I have a simple way to make very long, easily remembered passwords. Take a sentence which is easy to remember such as 'I will travel to Europe.' For the password, write each word backwards followed by an increasing set of numbers, e.g., I1lliw2levart3ot4eporuE. If a punctuation symbol is required, you can add it at the end.

"I then ran out the door without even closing it and got into my car. Disk's car was there. Birch drove up but did not see me. He got out of his car and entered the apartment building. For all I knew, he was also there to kill me. I was afraid he would follow me, so I got out of my car and slashed one of his tires with my pocketknife.

"That is all I remember until I woke up flat on my back in front of the cabin. I had a cut on my head, and there was blood everywhere. Horse was next to me, and my bicycle saddlebags were there. Otherwise, I can't remember a thing about that day. Mostly I have been hiding out here waiting for my short-term memory to come back.

"One type of loss of memory from a traumatic brain injury (TBI) is called retrograde amnesia. It can last from a few minutes to a few weeks. On rare occasions it can last several months. I don't think mine is that severe, so I expect to get my memory back fairly soon. It generally only affects short-term memory. I have my long-term memory as you've seen."

"I carry a first aid kit with antibiotic ointment on my ATV. Do you need me to look at your buttock wounds?"

"Don't you wish! Sorry, that was an automatic response. Yes, it needs to be cleaned and dressed and checked for infection. But before you see my buttock, I need to see yours."

"Memory, if I had known we were going to play show-and-tell, I would have taken a shower."

"Hey, I have been bathing in the spring."

"Should we be talking about this in front of Signal? He's a juvenile, after all. I will pull down my pants over my butt. Memory, Signal is thumping."

"Yes, he is wondering what happened to your fur."

"If show and tell is over, I'll get the first aid kit and you go lie on your stomach on the bottom bunk."

"Hunter, frenzied railroad construction in the late 1800s across the American West guaranteed accidents were common and often fatal since medical care on the frontier was virtually nonexistent. Along the 1,300 mile stretch between St. Louis, Missouri, and El Paso, Texas, there was not one hospital. Around 12,000 railroad workers and operators died each year. When Robert Wood Johnson heard about this problem, he had the idea of packaging Johnson & Johnson's sterile surgical products in boxes that could be kept with railway workers to treat injuries, and the first aid kit was born. Eventually trains had to carry surgeons and medical cars to treat the railroad workers."

"Memory, with you around, I don't need an encyclopedia. We are ready. You will have to pull your pants down past your butt."

"Hunter, I hate the thought of you touching my buttock. I'd rather have a baby."

"We can do that, but you'll have to change positions."

"Weirdo. You'd better not stray too far from the two holes."

"Memory, do you mean the bullet holes?"

"Pervert. What are you doing back there?"

"I am certainly not looking for your library card. Let me take off the bandage. This looks terrible. It must be infected."

"No, that's just pine sap."

"Memory, pine sap?"

"Yes, it was the only antiseptic I had."

"Memory, let me use the whiskey to get this pine sap off. This may burn for a moment. Do you let everyone see your butt, or am I special?"

"Not even Signal has seen my buttock."

"The wound is clean. You did a good job of preventing infection. I'll put on some antibiotic ointment and a couple of bandages. It should be fine after this. There, just like new."

"Hunter, this is probably the closest either of us has ever come to having sex."

"Memory, they say you'll never forget your first time."

"It was good for me. How was it for you, Hunter?"

"Exhausting. Once is enough, for now."

"Hunter, you had better not tell anyone you've seen my buttock."

"Darn, I was going to put it on my webpage."

"Do you mean your animal husbandry webpage?"

"How do you know I have an animal husbandry webpage?"

"That wasn't hard to guess."

"Memory, does this make us bosom buddies?"

"No, buttock buddies. I need clothes."

"You are about my size, Memory. I will bring you some of my clothes tomorrow. I brought us turkey sandwiches and potato salad for lunch, and some extra sandwiches for your dinner. I also brought a thermos of coffee so you can keep the thermos to use later. I'm not used to eating lunch with someone. It's fun."

"Thank you for taking care of me, Hunter. These sandwiches are great."

"Memory, I need to go. I will come back tomorrow with your clothes."

"How can you come here so often? Don't you have to take care of your ranch?"

"No, I have four ranch hands who take care the ranch. They have worked for my family for years and don't need me to tell them what to do. They assume I am off doing ranch stuff."

"Hunter, I have wondered, what do sheep count when they want to go to sleep?"

"Never thought about it. I'm off. See you tomorrow."

"Signal, Hunter is gone. He is quite amazing. I can't believe he never told me who he was."

I made four sketches yesterday, but I have been here eight days. So today I will sketch the other four. This really does get my mind off my situation. It requires too much concentration for my mind to wander. Six hours went by very fast. That was tiring. I should eat my sandwiches and potato salad and go to bed. Signal, here are some dandelions.

Oh no. It is very late, and Signal is thumping again. Someone could be here. Grab the bow and arrow and turn the table on its side. I can't ever seem to get comfortable. I better call Hunter.

"Hunter, Signal is thumping again. Someone may be here."

"Memory, get behind the table with your bow and arrow and hornet spray. I am on my way out the door and will be there quickly. Stay on the phone so I know what's going on. Jump on my ATV and put the rifle between my legs. I know this is an emergency, and I have to go fast. Made it. I don't see anyone. Open the door, Memory."

"Hunter, Signal is still thumping, and my heart is racing. What do you think it is?"

"Let me check Signal. Memory, you gave Signal dandelions and did not remove the stems. They are extremely sour, and Signal is protesting that you gave him such awful stuff since he trusts you to only give him good food. I will remove the stems from the greens. I made us a rack of lamb this afternoon, and I grabbed it on the way out the door. I dry rubbed it and put it in a low-temperature 275-degree oven for four hours. Now the meat is falling off the bones. They are wrapped in foil so we can reheat them outside tomorrow. Let me put them in the cooler. We are both very upset, so I better sleep here tonight. Memory, why are you biting your lip?"

"No male has ever seen or touched my body. It's disconcerting. But thank you for fixing my wounds."

"I never expected to get this lucky so quickly."

"You call working on my butt 'getting lucky'?"

"It exceeded my wildest dreams."

"You don't have enough imagination, Hunter." God, I wish I had not said that.

"I do now. This has been a complete education for my imagination."

"Well, you better keep it in your head and off of me."

"Memory, no female has ever seen my butt before either. You are privileged."

"I will take this knowledge to the grave with me. I haven't told you, but my parents and grandparents left me an inheritance, which I will collect either when I get married or when I turn twenty-five."

"What is it?"

"I don't know. They just left me a safe deposit box key. Hunter, it's a good feeling to know that someone cares this much about me."

"You are my main concern. I doubt either of us will sleep well tonight."

"We have become unusually close in a short period of time, Hunter. What does that mean?"

"It was clearly meant to be."

"Where is this going?"

"Let it take its own course."

"Let's try to go to sleep. I will take the bottom bunk. Put the stuff on the top bunk under the bottom bunk. Good night, Hunter."

"Good night, Memory."

9

Outrunning a Bear

"Time for everyone to get up. Signal, here's your breakfast and water. You are moving around really well. You still like to poop in the corner. It has the advantage that I don't have to replace your moss. Let me scoop them up and throw them next to the cabin."

"Hunter, I made a kettle of hot water for coffee and pancakes with maple syrup for breakfast in a skillet on the grill. Everything is on the picnic table."

"This is a great meal, Memory. It's fun eating at the picnic table. Life everywhere."

"Hunter, now that we've eaten, cleanup is easy since the skillet does not really need cleaning, so I only have to wash off the plates and utensils in the basin with some of the leftover hot water and put the rest in the thermos."

"Memory, last night was terrible. I haven't been able to get you off my mind. And there was something you said. You said you went to college at twelve years old. How is that possible?"

"Yes, I earned PhDs in computer engineering and mathematics when I was eighteen, from MIT. At twenty-three I became the youngest full professor in the history of the University of Missouri. I am also a Curators Distinguished Professor."

"How old are you?"

"Twenty-three."

"I am also twenty-three. How could you have made it so far so fast?"

"I was born with a cross between an eidetic memory and hyperthymesia, plus a high IQ, whatever that means. An eidetic memory is commonly called a photographic memory. Hyperthymesia is the ability to remember almost every experience of your life, including what you have seen and read. This life of mine has been strange, and I usually do not share any of it with anyone. For example, at age fourteen months I was already talking in complete sentences. Everywhere my parents took me—like gas stations, stores, or restaurants—I would ask where they slept and where their beds were. Since I was freakishly tall for my age and they could understand me, they thought I was much older and would answer that they have a house where they lived, and this was just where they worked.

"My parents were high school teachers, and my father was a coach. My mother couldn't brag about any of my milestones because no one ever believed her. So she just stopped discussing me with other mothers. Once she put me down in my crib for a nap and went outside to hang laundry. I carefully piled up everything in my crib, climbed on the pile, and escaped. When my mother saw me outside, she turned white and looked afraid. I asked her what she was doing and could I help. She was adamant that I was to never go outside by myself. Her expressions and harshness were hard on me. When I washed dishes, my parents would put something on the counter for me to read, so this was a learning experience.

"Skipping ahead quite a bit, on the first day of kindergarten, my mother walked me to school. As soon as we reached the school grounds, I took off and said, 'I can take it from here.' When she picked me up after school that day, I proudly said, 'You were the only mother not there this morning.' My mother said she was embarrassed because everyone might think she was a bad mother, but I was proud.

"Most people seem to think it would be wonderful to be ahead of everyone at school and to have a great memory. It was torture, even in grade school. My parents already had me reading newspapers and books to them, so the reading material at school in first grade was unbelievably simple and boring. I asked the teacher if there were better books we could read. She complained to my parents, who explained my situation. Then I was given many different tests and moved up several grades. The older kids did not like me in their classes one bit. That is when I had my first experiences with being bullied. So my father enrolled me in martial arts classes at age six. I've been taking them ever since.

At age seven, I lost my parents. They were killed by a drunk driver on the way home from their anniversary dinner."

"I am so sorry you had to deal with that, Memory."

"Unfortunately, Hunter, I didn't have any siblings to discuss things with, since I am an only child."

"I am also an only child. Sorry to interrupt. Go on."

"My grandparents took me in. With money from my parents' life insurance and settlement from the accident, they decided Grandma could quit her job and homeschool me. My grandparents lived with my great-grandparents, who owned a large ranch. When my grandmother's mother died, she left the ranch and this land to my grandmother. My grandparents sold off that ranch and became somewhat wealthy. They then moved to town but kept a horse trailer and some horses at a local stable.

"Since they were used to being on a ranch, fifty years ago my grandparents built this cabin as a summer home. Everything was brought in by horse. They moved Osage orange saplings to make a fenced pasture area. As you certainly know, the fruit of these trees are wrinkled green balls the size of grapefruits, called hedge apples. These trees bear long, tough thorns, sharp as steel. Osages grow fast, and in a few years form a hedge almost tight enough to hold water. Any spaces between trees was screened by thick thorny branches. If planted close together, Osages only grow twenty to thirty feet tall, so they do not shade the crops. These trees were used for the hubs and rims of wheels on wagons since its great strength allowed it to bear heavy loads, while its flexibility made it easy to bend into the circle of a wheel rim. It also had the capacity to absorb shock without cracking or splitting."

"You are just a wealth of information, Memory."

"Sorry, my memory just spills out. For the first five years, the horses were tethered to a pole in the pasture when they were not being ridden, which had to be moved often. Then they had the pack horses draw a trailer with wood for the gate and the floor of the cabin, which was dirt until then.

"Over time, my grandparents brought the stove, shakes to replace the sod roof, and screens for the windows. When I was little, we would all spend our summers here at the cabin. They'd let me do anything and everything. In mornings I'd listen before opening my eyes. When I heard birds chirping, I'd jump out of bed and run outside. It was an incredible experience to live here. We'd play horseshoes with both real horseshoes and then modern horseshoes, which are much larger. We'd collect rocks, arrowheads, and sometimes pan for gold in the creek, which in Missouri is really just gold flour. We had a picnic table of cedar, but after thirty years, it disintegrated. We'd ride horses. Grandpa had a tandem saddle so I could ride with him at first.

"We'd collect cattail parts and various greens to eat. We'd fish and swim in the creek. They fixed the spring, so water was easier to get every day. We'd come once before school was over to plant potatoes and tomatoes in the garden spot after the last freeze. We mounded the dirt in rows with ditches in between the rows, so watering was more efficient. About every two weeks, Grandpa would go to town. He would take the laundry to be done, the trash, and get supplies. We also read a lot. I hated to leave at the end of the summer.

"Then my education progressed very rapidly. We quickly made it through the eighth-grade curriculum. So I was doing high school work at age ten and took courses at the local community college in mathematics, chemistry, and physics. I was ready for college at age twelve. I didn't have to apply to college since I got the highest-possible score on both the SAT and ACT. So twelve colleges applied to me. I eventually went to the University of Missouri so my grandparents could keep an eye on me. They would have preferred that I commuted to school, but at twelve, I could not drive. So they put me in a dorm.

"You cannot imagine what it is like to go to college at age twelve. For one, since I was homeschooled, I missed the experience of four years of high school. This is where everyone learns social interaction. So when I arrived in college, I didn't have common experiences with the other students and didn't know how to interact with them. I didn't even know any slang terms. I was an outcast at first. They were always saying things I did not understand, or they were tricking me. They were obsessed with sex talk. I found ways to get away from them and never went out with them. Luckily, the drinking age in Missouri has been twenty-one since 1945. So I didn't have to go to bars.

"One Saturday, they talked me into going with them to a fraternity party.

"I thought they would play games, dance, blow up balloons, and have fun. Actually, it was a nightmare. All they did was drink and do small talk or sex talk. My friends introduced me to a group of males. I didn't know it, but all they had on their minds was how they could get a twelve-year-old into bed. Perverts.

"One said, 'Why do you always dress so completely from head to toe?'

I replied, 'How did you get into college without having any imagination?' Then he said, 'Do you know anything about sex?'

"I replied facetiously, 'Only what I read in the newspapers.' He replied, 'Do you want to learn?'

"So I came at him with, 'I have read a dozen books on it. I doubt that you know enough to teach me anything new.'

"He said, 'At least I have done it.'

"I said, 'Unfortunately for you, I do have a good imagination. You could not do anything but disappoint.'

"He got defensive and wondered if I was a lesbian and said, 'Do you like men?'

"My comeback: 'Don't know. I have met many males in college, but I have yet to meet a man.'

"My friend cut in, 'Tim, can't you tell when you are outmatched by a twelve-year-old?'

"After that, people treated me with more respect."

"Memory, this is an incredible story. See, you knew how to banter even at age twelve. I am glad you are not twelve years old now, since I am not a pedophile."

"Are you saying you are also thinking about getting me into bed, Hunter?"

"It's the thought that counts, Memory."

"Maybe you need to clean up your thoughts, Hunter."

"Then what would I do for excitement?"

"Is the thought of sex the only thing exciting for you?"

"Only since I met you, Memory."

"You are beginning to scare me again, Hunter."

"Memory, you know I am just having fun bantering so I can see that cute little expression you get when you are frustrated. Let's take a break and get lunch started. We can put the rack of lamb on the grill and continue your story."

"I could have graduated from the university in two years, but I was having so much fun being around an exciting learning environment and lab classes that I decided to stay an extra year just to take more courses. I had three majors: computer engineering, mathematics, and psychology. I took psychology since I was too young to understand what was going on around me. I also took biology, chemistry, and physics.

"There are over 23,000 higher-education institutions in the world, 4,360 in the US. Of these, 2,832 are 4-year colleges. The US has 16 million college students. MIT is consistently ranked with Harvard as the top two universities in the world. So when I graduated at 15 from the University of Missouri, I went to MIT for graduate school since it is the world leader in computer engineering and mathematics. Sorry, my memory just dribbles out.

"My grandparents set me up with a bank account, a furnished apartment, and they signed the lease. Housing is very sparse and expensive in Boston, so I advertised in the papers for a roommate. The person who answered the ad was Dorsa, who was working on a PhD in Psychology at Harvard. MIT does not have a degree in psychology. So I read every psychology book she brought home. I was probably eligible for a PhD in psychology but was not about to enroll in Harvard also. I managed to graduate with two PhDs in three years.

"I could have gone anywhere for a job, but I came back to the University of Missouri because my grandparents were old and needed some looking after. It was a short drive to their new home in Jefferson City. I talked Dorsa into coming to the University of Missouri.

"I was excited to get into academia so I could work with others to advance my fields. Unfortunately, I discovered that we were not working together to advance our fields. We were working to advance ourselves. This comes with the territory. We are competing for jobs, promotion, tenure, grants, etc. So to get ahead you have to outpace the others."

"Memory, this is similar to a story they told when I was in the boy scouts. Two scouts are out hiking, and they see a bear charging at them across a field. One scout turns to run. The second scout sits down and takes his running shoes out of his backpack. The other scout says, 'Why are you putting on running shoes? You can't outrun a bear.' The second scout responds, 'I don't have to outrun the bear. I just have to outrun you.'"

"But I outran the others, Hunter. I wrote forty papers in five years and, as I told you, this year at twenty-three I became the youngest full professor in the history of the University of Missouri, and I'm also a Curators Distinguished Professor. That is why some people at the university nicknamed me Brain. So now you have my story."

"This is unbelievable, Memory. I don't know how to absorb all of this. When I do, I'll have a million questions. So I guess you did not have a Barbie doll as a kid?"

"No, but I decided if I did it would have to be Divorce Barbie since she comes with all of Ken's stuff."

"Cute, Memory."

"What is your story, Hunter?"

"Let's eat lunch at the picnic table, and I will tell you my story another day."

"Hunter, this rack of lamb is delicious. It really does fall off the bones. Thank you, so much."

"MEMORY" SURVIVAL

"You are welcome. I listened to the news last night. Not much new. As you know, the police found your car in the Missouri river. Since they found hair in the cracked windshield, they think you might have drowned, and are searching the river."

"I don't remember any of that, Hunter."

"Memory, I have to go but will be back tomorrow with your clothes and bring horseshoes. So I can relax, from now on, call me on the phone when you go to bed."

"I look forward to seeing you tomorrow, Hunter."

It is hard to control my thoughts about my situation. Maybe I will write a "score" this afternoon to use up the time. I can take the music paper and put my "piano" on the table and practice it. It took an hour to write just one page. Let me try it on my piano. Now for page 2. At least this has gotten my mind off my situation. That used up the afternoon. Let me eat leftover lamb. Even cold, it is good. I need to call Hunter.

"Hi, Hunter. Perhaps we can talk a little."

"Sounds good. What would you like to talk about?"

"I've never had a real friend or someone who cares about me enough to make sure I am safe every day. It's a wonderful feeling."

"I've never had a real friend either, Memory. I love every minute I get to spend with you."

"Me too, Hunter. It gives me something to look forward to every day. Especially in this confusing circumstance."

"I am really impressed at how well you are dealing with this situation. I don't think I could handle it so well."

"Sometimes it just feels overwhelming. And not remembering makes it even more frightening."

"I will always be here for you."

"Thanks, Hunter."

"Memory, I saw some math notes on your shelf. Was that your research?"

"Yes, I am doing research on AI. Today more and more decisions are being made by artificial intelligence systems. I am looking for a mathematical means to help eliminate biases in AI systems, which tend to have biases towards making unethical and potentially very costly and damaging choices. Also, in one study, they had the computer scour the internet for information. It quickly became racist and sexist since it stores everything it finds. I need to figure out how to get the computer to recognize when it has phony information and store it someplace where it does not control current decisions. I have made progress on this research but have a long way to go."

"That is very interesting. Memory, tomorrow I will bring you new clothes. Wearing bloody clothes does not really fit the handbook of 'how to dress for success.'"

"Are you saying you do not like my clothes, Hunter?"

"I love your clothes. The two bullet holes in the back of your pants gives a glimpse at that perfect butt."

"So I am a peepshow to you."

"That and a lot more, Memory."

"I am afraid to ask what 'a lot more' means."

"At least your brilliant brain is always fully exposed. I will seek solace from that."

"Think more about my brain, Hunter."

"Sometimes when you giggle, you seem to be twelve again, Memory."

"What do other people do, practice giggling in the mirror?"

"But they will never be as cute as you."

"Are you are just bantering again, Hunter?"

"Actually, teasing is a form of flirting, Memory."

"So now you are flirting with me?"

"Someone has to, Memory. You have no idea what flirting is."

"So you have decided it is your job to educate me?"

"You know so much it is almost impossible for someone to teach you something new. I just couldn't pass up the opportunity."

"Hunter, I think I can sleep now."

"Sweet dreams, Memory."

"See you in the morning, Hunter."

"Signal. Here are some greens and carrots. You still have pellets left. I will fill your water bowl. Now I am off to bed."

10

Eidetic Memory

"Signal, what are you doing on my bed? I guess your hind legs have all their strength, but you couldn't jump off because you'd have to land on your front paws. I will pick you up and put you on the floor. I can't cuddle you since you must stay wild and be fearful of humans and other animals. Thank goodness for the fan. It was very hot last night. Let's get moving before Hunter arrives. This morning with your breakfast, I'll give you some honey-nut Cheerios. Wow! You're really attacking the Cheerios. I'll also have Cheerios and put the kettle on the grill for coffee."

Hearing that the police are searching the Missouri river for me has brought back another part of my memory. I need to tell Hunter. He is really obsessed with sex. I need to try to keep pointing him in another direction.

I will open the shutters and go wash up in the spring. I can bring some soap and a towel in my backpack, the water jugs to be filled, and carrots for Horse. Another great day. The walk to the spring is full of life.

"Hello, Horse. I brought you some carrots. Let me pet your head and rub your nose. I need to come and ride you. I'm not quite ready for this yet, but I will be by regularly to see how you're doing."

The spring water is cold. It certainly wakes you up. Let me fill the water jugs. I will carry the jugs back to the cabin in my hands. Got home in a flash. Wow. Did I just call this place home? Strange.

This is my life now. What a mess. But somehow, thanks to Hunter, it does not seem all bad. Maybe things are not as bleak as they first seemed. I have proven to myself that, if necessary, I can survive here alone in the woods. And if I hadn't been stuck here, I never would have met Hunter. This situation allowed me to enjoy Horse and Signal, along with all the wonderful creatures of the woods.

There is a lot of beauty here in the wilderness that I hadn't thought about in a while. I've enjoyed sunrises, sunsets, and many other sights, sounds, smells, and tastes that I have been oblivious to far too long. Meeting Hunter seems to have altered my entire life. He's the most special person I've ever encountered. I can't imagine life without him. Hunter is here. Put hot water in the thermos.

"Hi, Hunter. Would you like a mug of coffee?"

"Sure. I brought one of my drones and the controller. We can keep them on the shelf, so if we think someone is around, we can search for them. Here are three sets of my clothes: three pairs of jogging pants with zipper pockets and a drawstring so you will not need a belt, two cowboy snap shirts, one pullover, and socks. They should fit. I brought rubber boots for rainy days and your trips to the spring and creek. You can put the clothes on the clothes hooks. I also brought sandwiches and potato salad."

"Very thoughtful of you, thanks. Another part of my memory has returned."

"Tell me."

"After I slashed Birch's tire, I took off in my car, driving carefully since I could not afford to get stopped. I left town and got on I70 going west. Suddenly, Birch was coming up behind me. He was in Disk's car. Discovering he had a flat tire, he must have gone back in and grabbed Disk's car fob. Luckily, today, throughout your car are various computers called electronic control units (ECUs). Every car has up to one hundred semiconductor chips, and electric cars may have three thousand. Any computer can be hacked. As I have a PhD in computer engineering, with a little effort, I hacked Disk's car and used my cell phone to set off Disk's airbags and turn the engine off. Birch was fading into the background, but I had to get off the interstate since he had probably called the state police. I needed to get someplace safe so I could figure all this out, and I did not want them to find me.

"I found a side road off the interstate which goes down to the Missouri River. At 2,341 miles, the Missouri river is the longest river in North America. It starts just west of Bozeman, Montana, where the Gallatin, Jefferson, and Madison rivers converge at three forks. A quarter mile from the river, I stopped and took my window hammer out of the console, cracked the windshield, and stuck some of my hair into it. I turned off my cell phone and put it, my wallet, and the car fob in Faraday bags and then into the saddlebags. I then threw the saddlebags out next to the car and rolled down the windows.

"Next, I drove the car into the river. I knew when the police found it and saw my hair stuck in the cracked windshield they would think I hit my head on the windshield and drowned. That is all I remember."

"Why didn't the airbags go off, Memory?"

"When my grandparents sold the farm, they gave me one of their old cars without airbags. Airbags were not required in cars until 1998, and this is an older model."

"Hopefully, you will get the rest of your memory back soon. You told me a little about having an eidetic memory and hyperthymesia. Can you tell me more?"

"This is as much a curse as anything. The good parts include the fact that you don't lose things. You always know where your car fob is, the TV remote, or where something is that you put away a year or more ago. The advantages of having a strong memory are infinite. You can easily memorize new information and keep it in your brain. I can vividly recall sights, sounds, smells, tastes, and other sensations in detail. Without even concentrating, I can visualize people I have seen years ago for just five minutes. I can even recall such small details as hair, accents, mannerisms, speech patterns, behaviors, clothing, etc.

"Imagine being able to remember every painting, on every wall, in twenty museums I visited while traveling and lecturing. For most people, memory is a kind of scrapbook, a mess of blurred and faded snapshots of our lives. My memory is like a library of VHS tapes,

DVD movies, and streaming video walkthroughs of every day of my life from waking to sleeping. My memory is a running movie that never stops. I see the world in split screens, with the past constantly playing at the same time as the present. It is extremely difficult to concentrate since every event I encounter is running parallel to my memory of the historical and other events related to it. I store all this as separate capsules in my brain. Most of the time I can keep them separated, but occasionally, some capsules leak and merge into a living nightmare.

"For most people, as much as they would like to cling onto some of their past, even the most pertinent moments can be washed away with time. The human mind is probably designed to forget for a reason. For one, to get rid of unhappy memories. The brain can become overloaded with lots of unneeded information. Forgetting makes our brains more efficient. Memory involves selecting bits of information we need while ignoring what's unnecessary. Remembering what someone looks like is beneficial. Remembering exactly what they were wearing each and every time you met them is not. Hyperthymesia is not as simple as complete autobiographical recall. It is almost as if you never stop living every experience you've ever had. Emotions never wane. Details never fade. Time never, ever heals. Life is a perpetual open wound at times. People with a weak memory do not encounter this problem. They wish they had a good memory to remember things. I just wish I could forget some things sometimes.

"For me, it is very hard to forget embarrassing moments. You feel the same emotions—it's just as raw, just as fresh. It's nearly impossible to turn off that stream of memories no matter how hard you try. I will never forget when I was two years old and my father took me to the store. I saw bubble gum on the bottom shelf and took a piece since I didn't know you had to pay for things. When we left, my father saw it and asked how I got it. It was the first time he was gruff with me and took me back in the store to return the gum. The storeowner said he was impressed that I apologized, and gave me the gum for free. But I will carry the bad memory in an isolated capsule forever. After that, my parents gave me a piggybank and started giving me an allowance of $5 a week for chores.

"People often refer to the 'learning curve.' But much more important is the 'forgetting curve.' Cramming for a test may get you to pass, but very little of that information will be long lasting. Perhaps the most famous example of the forgetting curve occurred on 25 February 1988, when at a performance in Worcester, Massachusetts, Bruce Springsteen forgot the opening lines to his all-time greatest hit 'Born to Run'. This seems impossible since he had sung this song thousands of times. At a loss for why this happened, he told the audience, 'Sung it so damn much I forgot what the words were.' There has been an enormous amount of research on the forgetting curve going back to the 1800s. But we still have a long way to go to a full understanding of it."

"You are drowning in information as usual, Memory. If you have sex, you will have some good memories to offset the negative ones."

"I think I can find good memories which do not involve sex, Hunter."

"Or maybe they will be so good that they will also become distracting, Memory."

"What have you got in mind, Hunter?"

"I am just trying to help you, Memory."

"You are just trying to help yourself, Hunter."

"God helps those who help themselves, Memory."

"I don't think that is what that expression means, Hunter."

"Creative thinking is always good, Memory. But I am patient."

"You had better have infinite patience, Hunter."

"Sorry for pushing your buttons again, Memory. But I love the look on your face when frustrated. Continue with your story."

"Another problem that happens now and then is when I remember things other people can't. They say it never happened because they just don't remember. They seem to get pretty upset sometimes, like they think I'm just making it up. People who have a weak memory may completely forget about something in their past. Usually, these people are happier than people who have strong memory. This is probably where the adage 'Ignorance is bliss' comes from. It is necessary to have good emotions in order to be happy. Consequently, you won't be able to feel happy if you constantly remind yourself of past mistakes you have made. So I try to never remember anything bad. My bad memories are tucked away in memory capsules which occasionally leak out. Also, when people can't understand you, can't relate to you, and are afraid of your memory, they can be cruel."

"Quite a story, Memory. How do you store it if you tell a lie?"

"I cannot tell a lie. I must be able to trust that any memory I have is real and true."

"Can we test your memory? What did I say to you the first time we met five days ago?"

"I said, 'What are you doing here?' You said, 'I own the ranch on the west side of this property. My name is Hunter.' I said, 'So you left the $10 bill and a note by the whiskey bottle.' You said, 'Yes, last fall.' I said, 'My grandparents call me Memory. This is their cabin. So what are you doing here?' You said, 'I raise sheep, and the coyotes have been killing them. I asked your grandfather if I could hunt them on his land, and he said it was fine. He said he had his wife and granddaughter here with him.

"I said, 'Llamas can be used as guards against coyote attacks on sheep herds. Just one guard llama is an effective protector of a small herd and can even kill an attacking coyote.' You said, 'Why did they not teach me that in AG school? Thank you so much for that information.'"

"Okay. I get the point, Memory. You have total recall. Remind me to never argue with you."

"Hunter, that was five days ago, not five *years* ago."

"Five days ago is five years ago for me."

"A minute ago for me, Hunter. Amazingly disturbing, isn't it?"

"You seem remarkably well adjusted for carrying such a burden."

"Thanks, Hunter."

"Do you know everything about everything?"

"No, like the average person, I don't know much about most things."

"What don't you know?"

"For one, I don't know a good synonym for *thesaurus*."

"What is one of the most surprising things you've learned?"

"There are many, but for one, I always knew that blue whales are the largest living mammals—even larger than most dinosaurs. The biggest blue whales can be over one hundred feet in length and weigh more than one hundred tons. Their hearts alone can weigh one thousand three hundred pounds and are the size of a small car. The beating of their hearts can be heard two miles away. Not surprisingly, blue whales have enormous arteries, which pump blood through their massive hearts and into their vital organs. Here's the surprise: these arteries are so big that a fully grown human could swim through them. Add to that the fact that a baby blue whale may gain two hundred pounds a day during its first year."

"That is certainly surprising. We can have sandwiches and potato salad for lunch. I'll have roast beef and cheese with mayonnaise. You?"

"Ham and cheese with no mayo works for me. I'll get out plates and forks."

"Memory, I won't cut the sandwiches. This is a nice lunch, and it is fun sitting outdoors with life all around us. I checked the news. The police have given up searching the river for you. They are no longer sure you drowned since they have been using GPS to locate your cell phone without success. Also, they brought in search dogs that followed your scent away from the river and then lost it. So they are beginning to think you are alive."

"Hopefully, the police cannot find me even if they suspect I am alive."

"Memory, to be safe, I will make sure no one is following me when I come here. Let's play a friendly game of noncompetitive horseshoes. I see there are already two white posts in the ground."

"Hunter, I will go first. These horseshoes are about two pounds. I am going to try to flip mine in the air with my pitch. It flipped once in the air and landed really close to the stake. Next, I will hold one on the side and try to slide it onto the stake. Close again. Now it is your turn."

"Both of yours are close enough to the stake for a point each. I will try to get a ringer, or at least closer to the stake than yours. That one looks really close. Here's my next try. Let's go down there and see who is closest."

"Hunter, it looks like we both have two horseshoes equally close to the stake. Let's try again in the other direction. This time, I got a ringer. That's three points. Maybe I can get another ringer. No, but close. Your turn, Hunter."

"I didn't get a ringer, but I am closer than your next nearest one. Try again. Ringer! The game is tied. That was fun."

"Hunter, did you hear that? Horse is trying to get our attention. He just whinnied. Now he's snorting. Usually he just sighs when I am petting him. Now he's pawing the ground with his front leg. It's almost like Signal's back-leg thump."

"Horse hears us playing outside. Let's go pet him and give him some carrots. Short trip to the pasture. Here are some carrots, Horse. Memory, let's go back to the cabin, and then I need to go. See you tomorrow, and I will give you my life's story."

"Bye, Hunter."

I need to occupy my time this afternoon. There are a few books on the shelf that I've not read. With Hunter fixated on sex, it might be interesting to read Bryan Sykes's *Adam's Curse*. This is interesting reading. A lot to digest. This used up the afternoon, but I really wanted to understand it.

Something that surprised me concerns the marine worm Bonellia viridis. You will never see a male since they actually live inside the female's womb, where he feeds on her nutrients, and only produces sperm when she is ready to lay eggs. Imagine a husband like that who is just a sperm delivery system, tucked away out of sight and reduced to a single function: fertilizing your eggs. What a world that would be.

"Signal, here is your dinner. I will have sandwiches and potato salad again. I will cut the sandwiches on the diagonal for a change. Ham and cheese is still my favorite. Hunter is really taking care of us. I don't know what I would do without him. I would probably end up eating snapping turtle, snakes, and insects. These sandwiches taste great. Hunter made a good choice. I don't like going outside in the dark, but I need to go to the outhouse. Be back soon, Signal."

*****

It is 9:00 p.m., and Memory has not called. I'd better call her. Oh no. She is not answering. Try again. No answer. This could be bad. I better get there in a hurry. Bring a flashlight, load my gun, and take off on the ATV. I better keep my gun between my legs since I may have to make a split-second decision.

This is a difficult trip in the dark, but the ATV has lights, and I need to get there in a hurry. My heart is pounding. I am scared something terrible has happened. Memory could be shot or kidnapped or who knows what. Why am I talking to myself out loud? It is a consequence of dire panic. Made it to the cabin. Grab the gun and run inside. No Memory.

"Signal, where is Memory?" Why the hell am I asking Signal?

Go back outside and call loudly, "Memory!" Run toward the pasture. "Memory, where are you?"

"Hunter, I am up here in an oak tree. Coyotes all around."

"Memory, I see four coyotes under the tree. Four quick shots, and they are dead. Memory, you can come down."

"I am lucky it was not a bear, or he would be up here in the tree with me. Let me get down."

"Wow! You look beautiful even in my clothes, Memory. Did they bite or scratch you? I don't want to worry about rabies."

"No, I wasn't cut. That was a close call. You know that 'up a tree' means 'in a difficult situation without escape, cornered.'"

"Quite appropriate, Memory. Why were you out here at night?"

"It was dusk, but I had to go to the outhouse. When I left the outhouse, a pack of coyotes came at me. I hadn't noticed that there was a rabbit behind me. I thought they were coming at me. I had a can of hornet spray, but when they startled me, I dropped it and had to run for the nearest tree. My only chance was to climb this oak tree, which has a huge grapevine wrapped around the trunk. That was impressive shooting in the dark, Hunter. What do we do with the four dead coyotes?"

"Their pelts are worth $100 each. I will take them back with me when I go home. Memory, coyotes are nocturnal hunters by nature, making dawn and dusk their optimal hunting times as they look for food. Coyotes very rarely attack humans. Golf balls kill more people every year than coyotes. But running from them can trigger a coyote's prey drive and cause them to chase you. That is probably what happened here. Memory, the hair is sticking up on the back of your neck, and you are covered in goosebumps."

"That was a terrifying experience, Hunter."

"I was also terrified that something had happened to you, Memory. You are now my whole life. It will take me awhile to get over this nightmare. Let me sleep here tonight so I can relax knowing you are safe."

"I have a leg cramp from being in the tree so long. I am not sure I can walk."

"I have to carry my gun, so you grab your hornet spray, climb on my back, and I will carry you back to the cabin. Let's get in the cabin."

"That was actually fun, Hunter."

"I can take the top bunk since you have a leg cramp."

"Hunter, it will be difficult for me to go to sleep."

"Me also, Memory. Perhaps we can talk for a moment. From now on, don't ever leave the cabin without your cell phone in your zipper pocket please. Memory, is this a date?"

"Depends. Are you married?"

"Never had the desire."

"Me either. Hunter, do you date?"

"No. The sheep get jealous if they see me with a woman. Do you date?"

"I did once and was lucky to get out alive."

"Memory, perhaps we could date sometime."

"But first, I would have to meet your sheep, Hunter."

"Memory, do I need Signal's permission?"

"Definitely."

"Memory, you know that today some people expect to have sex on a first date."

"You will still be expecting that long after I'm gone, Hunter."

"I was just hoping to get lucky."

"Hunter, you will never be that lucky."

"So what do I have to look forward to?"

"Surviving, as long as you keep your hands off me."

"That seems a little harsh."

"Hunter, you are the one who likes bantering. Don't you like it coming back at you?"

"I never met someone brilliant enough to take me on. Besides, sex is natural."

"For rabbits maybe. Why did you send us in this direction?"

"Sorry, for me it comes naturally around you, like breathing, even in the face of disaster. Memory, if I could remember all of my experiences, it seems impossible to deal with. Are you ever frightened?"

"Yes, Hunter. Having a superior autobiographical memory can be annoying to a lot of people, so sometimes I'll ask leading questions so they can participate in recalling something along with me. Memories occasionally do terrify me, which is why I developed the brain capsules technique to keep them under some control."

"Your memories fascinate me."

"Perhaps we better go to sleep now. I am on the bottom bunk. Good night, Hunter."

"Let me climb up the ladder. Good night, Memory."

11

A Hunter's Life

Slept restlessly. "Get up Hunter."

"Memory, that was a terrible night's sleep. I hope we don't have to go through that very often. What a nightmare."

"Signal, here's your breakfast and some Cheerios. You are hopping again, so you can go home soon. I will make eggs, toast, and coffee outside for us. Hunter, tomorrow I need more milk, eggs, and bread. I am definitely looking forward to your story, but first let's eat."

"Having breakfast with you makes my day, Memory. This is a great breakfast—and nourishing. Give me your dirty clothes, and I will wash them."

"Hunter, time for you to play the random word game. I will give you my written list: female, student, room, bicycle, nothing, money, willing, barter, points, place, body, said, sorry, trying, quit."

"Can you repeat them back to me?"

"Let me look at this for a few minutes. Let me give you back the written list. I used your memory device. Let me repeat your list. The story I made up is 'A female student came to my room on a bicycle wearing nothing. She needs money and is willing to barter for it. She points to a place on her body. I said, 'Sorry, I am trying to quit.'"

"Perfect, but you are really obsessed with sex."

"You are the one who made a list of dirty words."

"There are no dirty words in my list."

"I guess I have a good imagination."

"I have an excellent imagination, but it does not go in that direction. Have you always been this way?"

"Just since I met you, Memory. See, you really are a good teacher."

"That's not my subject, Hunter."

"Too bad. I think you would be really good at it."

"Let's get off this and on to your life story."

"My life was different from yours. I went through grade school fine. I worked on my parents' ranch and joined 4H. I loved animals and took rabbits and sheep to competition and won a lot of medals. This is why I know so much about rabbits."

"Hunter, the name 4H is a reference to the occurrence of the initial letter *H* four times in the organization's original motto: 'Head, Heart, Hands, and Health.' This was later incorporated into the fuller pledge officially adopted in 1927. In the United States, the organization is administered by the National Institute of Food and Agriculture of the United States Department of Agriculture. Sorry to interrupt. Go on."

"In high school, everyone liked me, and I was class president. I was pretty smart and graduated in three years. I was valedictorian and gave a speech at graduation about Temple Grandin. She is an American scientist and animal behaviorist. She has been the main advocate for the humane treatment of livestock. Her insight into the minds of cattle taught her to value the changes in details to which animals are particularly sensitive, and to use her visualization skills to design thoughtful and humane animal-handling equipment. She designed over half the humane animal slaughter facilities, stock yards, and feed lots in North America. She understood that there were always going to be slaughterhouses, since these are not zoo animals and people eat them. The best she could do is make their treatment as humane as possible.

"Grandin is currently a consultant to the livestock industry. She was named a fellow of the American Society of Agricultural and Biological Engineers in 2009. Despite being autistic, she got a PhD in Animal Sciences from the University of Illinois. Time's list of the

100 most influential people in 2010 named her in the Heroes category. She is also world renowned for her work to help people with autism. She is currently a professor in Animal Sciences at Colorado State University."

"Hunter, what I particularly like about Temple Grandin is that she thinks in pictures. She translates both spoken and written words into full color movies. This allows her to design entire systems in her imagination. The first thing she did when she arrived at a feedlot was to put herself inside the cattle's heads and look out through their eyes. This allowed her to design all kinds of equipment and systems for handling cattle, hogs, and sheep during slaughter. Quite remarkable. Sorry I interrupted, continue."

"I then went to the University of Missouri and got a degree in Animal Sciences so I could take over my family's cattle ranch. In college, I kept mostly to myself. After graduation, I went on for an MBA. Then I took over the family ranch, and as I mentioned earlier, my parents moved to St. Louis. We own the ranch jointly. They no longer need to work since they have plenty of income from the ranch. As I said, we have two thousand acres of land, five thousand head of sheep, and one thousand acres of wheat. Our wheat is planted in the fall and harvested in the spring.

"There is a large white two-story farmhouse sitting in a half mile from the road. Next to it are two red barns with a fenced area in between for horses. We don't raise horses, they are just used around the ranch. There is a bunkhouse for two of the ranch hands completely equipped with bedrooms, kitchen, bathroom, and all the amenities of home. The other two ranch hands commute to work from their homes. The ranch hands are somewhat independent.

"There are two silos for storing wheat until it goes to market. We have millions of dollars of equipment, including combines, chisel plows, tractors, planting equipment, cultivators, ATVs, SUVs, cattle trucks with divided compartments to haul sheep, and grain trucks to haul wheat to the grain elevator. As I told you earlier, I changed it from a cattle ranch to a sheep ranch. Currently I do sheep research for the agriculture school at the University of Missouri.

"I have a ham radio. I can use it to scout out information about you. Ham radios can be tracked, but I will not stand out since I am often online talking to other sheep ranchers. And that is about it."

"How are sheep used in research, Hunter?"

"Sheep are used in medical research as models of human disease, including disorders such as hemophilia, asthma, Tay Sachs disease, kidney disease, and more. They are also used to test treatments for these diseases and for vaccine research. This also makes them a useful model for studying brain diseases such as Huntington's disease. They are used extensively in veterinary research, studies of digestion in ruminants, and research on the impact of farming on the environment. Sheep are frequently used as a model for cattle and other large mammals, as they are less expensive to keep and easier to breed."

"Who would have thought it, Hunter?"

"We have leftover sandwiches for lunch. After lunch, I have to go to the agriculture school at MU to file a report on my sheep research. I have a research appointment in the agriculture school."

"Thanks, Hunter. This is really delicious. I can clean up. I hope to get the rest of my short-term memory back soon. I need to know if someone else is trying to kill me so I can make a plan. Maybe we can discuss this tomorrow. This is all really weighing on me. I need something to get mind off it."

"Do you want me to look at your butt again? It should get your mind off problems."

"Is my buttock all that you think about?"

"No. I spare ten minutes a day to think about taking care of my ranch. I don't have an eidetic memory like you. So I have to review the greatest moment of my life over and over."

"Hunter, if working on my buttock was the greatest moment of your life, you need to get out more."

"But you are already a full-time job, Memory."

"We need to find something new to occupy your mind, Hunter."

"Are you sure you want to show me another part of your body? Memory, did you just say *pervert* in sign language? How do you know that?"

"I read your books on sign language. Some people would say you have a one-track mind."

"Are you sure I am not just a mind reader, Memory?"

"Hunter, it is clearly not my mind you are reading."

"I'm just working off my wish list."

"Why did you get us involved in such a bizarre discussion?"

"See, I got your mind off your problems, didn't I?"

"And you shifted it to perversion, Hunter. Thank you. Why are you always bantering about sex?"

"I like the challenge, and I like to see your reaction when I push your buttons. You are particularly beautiful when frustrated."

"I've almost never been frustrated. You are teaching me what it means."

"Wow! I bet you never thought I could teach you something new. I have to go. I need to consider staying here at night so I know you are safe. I will see you tomorrow. I'll grab up the four coyotes on the way."

"I want to put clay in the cracks of the cabin tomorrow. Would you please bring me a bucket and a trowel? Bye, Hunter."

He is right. My other problems are not occupying my mind. Hunter's fixation on bantering is. I need to go ride Horse. I'll bring some carrots.

"Hi, Horse. We will go riding today. Since I don't have a saddle, we better just ride in your pasture area. Getting up on you is quite a challenge. I can hold onto your mane while we ride. Don't gallop, or I might fall off. We have been around and around the pasture. That was fun. Let me slide off and go back to the cabin."

I need to check the radio. The police report that the dogs followed my scent to a slaughterhouse. This raises the question of whether or not I am still alive and hiding. So there is an all-out search for me since they believe I must still be in the neighborhood. And I do not remember a slaughterhouse. I wonder if that's where Horse came from. What a disaster.

I'll try to do research this afternoon. This will occupy my mind for a while. Math is great since it can be done in your head or on paper. It does not need a blackboard, a lab, or any other apparati. I like the mental gymnastics.

I made it through another day. I'm just stalling until I get the rest of my memory back.

Maybe I'll make spaghetti for dinner. I can boil water to cook the pasta and heat the sauce in a skillet on the grill. Mix the pasta and sauce and after eating put the leftovers in the cooler. That was a change. A really normal meal for me.

I better call Hunter.

"Hi, Hunter. Thank you for saving me from the coyotes. Your life story was very interesting."

"You are welcome. I love every minute I get to spend with you. It makes my day."

"Hunter, I love being around you also. This is all new for me. I was never so close to someone before. I haven't shared or disclosed to anyone else that my memory is so weird. Since it seemed to bother some people, I assumed it was an undesirable trait. But you don't seem to be bothered by my memory at all, and even ask me questions about it. It's a pleasant surprise. You've only really tested it once about the very beginning when we met. You're unique that way."

"I find your memory charming, and I very much like the way you answer my questions about it. It's enjoyable, learning about how you're able to deal with such a memory. Amazingly, you're very optimistic, listen to me, and ask questions, and I can see that you're really listening to me by the way you tilt your head and ask follow-up questions. It's refreshing. For someone who has achieved so much early success, you're surprisingly down-to-earth and very easy to talk to."

"Thanks, Hunter. I feel very safe around you, like I can share anything. Even though I say *pervert* quite a bit, you can tell that I don't really mean it, right? It's my way of trying to adjust to and participate in your frequent bantering, which doesn't really bother me. It's just new to me."

"Memory, tell me something I do not know."

"The current American flag was designed by a seventeen-year-old high school student, Bob Heft. He designed the flag in 1958 as a project for his junior-year history class. His design had fifty states although there were only forty-eight states at the time, since he was convinced that Hawaii and Alaska would become states. His teacher did not like the project and gave him a B-minus. Heft then sent his design to Washington, and when President Dwight D. Eisenhower called to tell him his was accepted, his teacher changed his grade to an A."

"Thanks. I certainly did not know that. Have a good night, Memory."

"Good night, Hunter. See you tomorrow."

"Signal. Here's your food and water. I am worn out and off to bed."

12

Chinking

Wow! Slept ten hours. I really needed that. That's the first good night's sleep I have had in quite a while.

"Signal, here's your breakfast."

I'll put a kettle of water on the grill. As it heats up, I'll do martial arts in front of the cabin. The term *martial arts* is derived from Latin and means "arts of Mars," as Mars was the Roman god of war. I will practice kickboxing since it keeps your opponent a good distance from you, and I have unusually long legs. It is good exercise and will get my mind off all this stuff. That was tiring.

Now I can make breakfast. My mind seems to be racing. Oh no! The rest of my short-term memory has returned. Probably from telling Hunter about my life, eidetic memory, and hearing the latest news from the police. Luckily, Hunter has arrived. I will have to tell him the last part of the story. I will just have coffee for breakfast.

"Hello, Hunter. Do you want a cup of coffee?"

"Yes, please. I washed your clothes and have them with me. My llamas arrived yesterday. We put them out with the sheep and gave them their own feeding trough. They like fruit for treats. Again, thank you for telling me about this. I brought the milk, eggs, and bread you wanted, two buckets, two trowels, work gloves for both of us, and carrots for Signal and Horse. I got a bucket of KFC with all the trimmings while in town yesterday. We can have it for lunch, and you will have plenty left over. I also brought ice for the cooler. Let's drain the water out of the cooler and fill it with ice and food. We can still leave the oranges out."

"Hunter, the first oranges weren't orange. Oranges are a hybrid of two citrus fruits: pomelo and mandarin. They originally came from Southeast Asia and were green. The green is due to chlorophyll produced on the peel of the orange to protect itself from sunburn. Oranges in warmer regions still stay green through maturity, so the bright orange you see in stores may be because they are exposed to ethylene gas, coated in wax, or even dyed. Also, oranges did not get their name from their color. The name came from ancient times where they came from a tree called the 'orange tree.' The word *orange* entered the English language in the 1300s, while its reference to the fruit didn't appear until the 1500s."

"You never disappoint with your abundant knowledge, Memory. We can take Signal's leg brace off. I brought my elbow-length leather gloves. You hold him, and I will remove the brace. Signal, quit fighting, we are trying to help. There, you are free. I set him on the floor, and he flew off. He just did a binky. That is when they jump high in the air and twist and turn out of happiness."

"Hunter, the rest of my short-term memory has returned."

"So what do you remember?"

"As I told you, I went to the Missouri river, rolled down the windows of the car, and drove it into the river. This made the car sink rapidly. I carefully crawled out of the window and swam to shore. I decided I had to go to my grandparents' cabin to hide out, but it is five miles in from the nearest road.

"A five hundred-mile circle around western Missouri contains thirty percent of the horses in the US. So it was a short walk carrying the heavy saddlebags over my shoulders to a local slaughterhouse. An overload of adrenaline was keeping me going. There was a corral of horses, so it was easy to coax one out. I adjusted the saddlebags to fit the horse and rode bareback the five miles slowly and carefully through the woods to the cabin. I knew the route well since I had taken it many times with my grandparents. Then I must have passed out from loss of blood from my bullet wounds, fell off Horse, and hit my head, causing temporary amnesia. At least I have my memory back."

"Memory, I listened to the news. The police no longer believe you drowned in the river. They have been using GPS to try to locate your cell phone without success, and the dogs followed your scent to the slaughterhouse. This has made them very suspicious."

"I know, I heard it on the radio. What should I do?"

"Since we do not know which campus cops are in on this or if the city police are in on this, we cannot go to the police right now."

"Won't you be in trouble for helping me?"

"I have already put my life in your hands. Besides, we are buttock buddies. Joined by the butt for life. We need to make a plan for your safety. We don't know if Disk has friends who are searching for you. So you may be in serious danger. Can anyone figure out you are here?"

"No, Hunter. This place is in the name of my maternal grandmother, so it will not show up on any web search for me. And I never told Dorsa about this place."

"The cabin seems safe, Memory."

"As you know, there are no windows, only shutters I can lock, and there is a barn door lock on the front door, which is impenetrable. Also, Signal is nocturnal and will thump if anyone comes around."

"But we still have to stay alert. If you are found, it could be deadly. Do you have access to the news?"

"I have an old crystal radio, but it has poor reception and is hard to hear."

"Okay. I will continue to listen to the radio and the nightly news to see what is going on with your case. I'll bring you a radio when I come back tomorrow. For now, we need to put clay between the cracks in the cabin."

"Hunter, this is important since right now someone could look between the logs and see me inside. This will take time and effort. Let's put on our work gloves. I will take the carrots in my bucket, you take your bucket and carry the shovel to the creek. We can give Horse the carrots on the way. Let me put on my rubber boots and cowboy hat. I have made this trip so much I think I could do it blindfolded. Hi, Horse. The grasses in your pasture smell fresh and aromatic. Hunter is here and brought you some carrots. I'll pet your head. You seem to be doing well. I will ride you again one day."

"Memory, it looks like there is some clay over here near the creek. Putting it in the buckets is easy. Carrying them is not. We can leave the shovel here. The buckets are really heavy filled with clay, and we may have to make several trips."

"Hunter, now that we are at the cabin, we can use the trowels to push the clay into the cracks between the logs. It should dry completely in a couple days. This is strenuous and time-consuming."

"Memory, we should have the KFC before making another trip. We can just eat it cold. You get some plates, and I will get the KFC, and we can eat at the picnic table. KFC did not send napkins, so I brought out a box of Kleenex."

"Hunter, Kleenex tissues were originally intended for gas masks. There was a cotton shortage during WW1 when they were used for filters in gas masks. So Kimberly-Clark developed a thin cotton substitute for the army. But the war ended before it was perfected. So the company made the material smoother and softer, and Kleenex facial tissue arose."

"Memory, information just dribbles off you. This meal is a pleasant change. It is fun eating at the picnic table."

"Hunter, ever since this terrible event happened, I have been having nightmares."

"If I am here and you have a nightmare, just jump in bed with me."

"For all you know, that is my nightmare, Hunter."

"That is impossible. I am irresistible."

"In your mind, Hunter. What I wanted to say was that last night for the first time I had a wonderful dream. We were face-to-face talking and paying complete attention to one another."

"I have the same dream, Memory. We are face-to-face talking and paying complete attention to one another—in the bathtub. A nightmare for me is us in the bathtub and you fully clothed."

"Hunter, you should know that your obsession with sex can be irritating and frustrating."

"So it's a twofer."

"Hunter, where did you learn to make the most bizzare seem normal?"

"That comes naturally to me around you, Memory. Enough rest. Time for another trip. It was a quick trip to the creek. Fill the buckets. Go back and fill in the cracks. This next trip, I will take the shovel back with us. Push the clay into the cracks. That was exhausting. We have some clay left over we can use to chink the outhouse."

"Hunter, the outhouse was easy. At least the time is flying by, so I am not thinking about my circumstance. Where did the day go?"

"Great job. I am off, Memory. Tomorrow I have a surprise for you, and maybe I will start staying here at night."

"What is it?"

"If I tell you, it will not be a surprise. Bye, Memory."

"Bye, Hunter. See you tomorrow."

I can have leftover chicken for dinner and then feed Signal.

I hear an ATV about a mile away. I wonder if Hunter is coming back.

Let me call him.

"Hi, Hunter. I hear an ATV in the distance. Are you on the way back?"

"Memory, I'm at home. You may be in grave danger. Grab your bow and arrows, the hornet spray, and go behind the cabin into the woods so you are hidden. Stay on the phone so I know what's going on."

"I am out the door, Hunter, and headed behind the cabin. My heart is racing. I have the hornet spray in my pocket, the bow and arrows and the phone in my hands."

"I am on the way on my ATV and have my gun. But if it's the police, we will just have to give up. Either way, this is incredibly scary. I am moving as fast as possible. I cannot lose you. You have become my whole life."

"Same for me, Hunter. I will do my best to make it. If it is one of Disk's friends, I will have to shoot him with an arrow. The big problem is whether or not I can tell who it is. Especially if the police are not in uniform. And I may have to make a split-second decision."

"Memory, if they do not identify themselves immediately as the police, defend yourself. I am already on the rustic road to your cabin. Oh, I see. There are some kids here on ATV's. Kids, this is private property, and you can't be here. Please go home."

"So I can go back in the cabin?"

"Yes, but I will still come. Tomorrow I will call their parents and tell them this area is too rustic for children to be driving ATVs here and this is private property. That should end this problem."

"I'm here, Memory. That was a terrifying experience. It is going to take a while to calm down. I better stay here again tonight."

"We can talk, Hunter."

"I don't know what I would do if something happened to you."

"You are special to me also, Hunter. I have never been this close to someone before. I don't know how to react to it."

"I'm going to have to start staying here every night. These nightly incidents are too terrifying. I am having trouble sleeping for worrying about you."

"That is not necessary, but you are welcome to stay here if you want."

"I might have to return to my ranch during the day, but I will come back at night."

"Do what makes you comfortable."

"Memory, do you have to try very hard to remember something you're trying to recall?"

"No, usually my brain just does that all by itself without my ever paying attention. Occasionally a letter or number might pop up out of nowhere and will prompt a sudden recall. Sometimes chunking occurs where clusters of related memories are all triggered at once."

"Memory, does the nickname Brain bother you?"

"No, Hunter. By reading a lot I am able to direct conversations away from me and on to interesting topics people can share. Since the nickname mostly refers to things I've read and not me personally, I think of Brain used in a teasing sense. Since I'm very private, I guard my memories and unusual life carefully. Sharing tidbits from reading was my way of interacting since I really didn't have much in common with others. I didn't know popular music, films, or other common topics. My life experiences were too different to share. I knew no slang and frequently didn't know what people were talking about."

"Well, Memory. You seem to have found a lot of uses for the word *pervert*."

"Hunter, we should try to go to sleep now. You can have the top bunk."

"Good night, Memory. I look forward to seeing you in the morning."

"Good night, Hunter."

13

Horsing Around

"Everybody, up. Here's your breakfast, Signal. I am making coffee and hot oatmeal for us to eat outside, Hunter. At least this is quick. Thank you for staying last night. I did not want to be alone. It's becoming scary here."

"Thanks for breakfast, Memory. I need to go but will be back shortly. I need to feed the cats and get your surprise. We have cats to keep mice out of the barns."

"Hunter, like most four-legged mammals, cats have five toes on their front feet. But on their back feet, they only have four toes. Scientists believe that helps them run faster. I am looking forward to my surprise."

"You never cease to amaze, Memory. I am off."

I'll clean up the cabin while he's gone. I already hear Hunter's ATV outside. Open the door.

"Hi, Hunter, why do you have a horse tied to the back of your ATV?"

"For your surprise, Memory, I will spend the whole day here, and we will go horseback riding together. My horse, Bolt, is saddled up. He's a quarter horse, which is the most popular breed in the United States. The compact body of the American quarter horse is well-suited for the intricate and quick maneuvers required in rounding up cattle and sheep. I brought a saddle pad, saddle, and bridle, which we call 'tack,' for Horse, plus water and sandwiches for lunch in my saddlebags. I brought a headlamp for me, and we can take yours in case darkness descends on us. I also brought a pair of my cowboy boots for you since they are much safer around horses. I brought a radio, a lantern, and BenGay. What is the BenGay for? Do you have pain someplace?"

"I sometimes put it on my forehead since the warmth seems to increase my concentration."

"I'll put this stuff on the table and close the shutters, Memory, and you grab up Signal. It is time for him to go home. You carry him to the creek."

"Let me set him down in front of your horse while I put on my new boots and get my cowboy hat."

"Memory, will he run off?"

"If he does, he will just run home anyway, Hunter. Wow! Signal is straight up on his hind legs and rubbing noses with Bolt. I have never seen that before."

"Memory, something else rabbits and horses have in common is that they both can sleep standing up and with their eyes open. I will take my ATV with your horse tack and Bolt to the pasture. I'll saddle up Horse while you take Signal to the creek."

Let me put the leaf in the door, grab up Signal, and take him home.

"Signal, you have been a good friend and companion. We've been through a lot together. I am really going to miss you, but it is time for you to get on with your life. We are at the creek. Bye, kid. Stop by anytime you feel like it."

Let me get on Horse.

"Hunter, ride towards the cabin. There is a trail behind the cabin through the woods."

"I see the trail, Memory. I am surprised that there is not much grass on the trail, and it feels like we are going into a tunnel."

"That's because of the tall sycamore trees on both sides of the trail. These massive trees have large white branches with broad leaves with shallow lobes. They have distinctive bark that sheds to reveal white bark underneath. Their upper branches are overhanging the trail, blocking out much of the sunlight. This casts strange shadows all around. There are logs, branches, twigs, fallen leaves, and undergrowth throughout this forest. This provides hiding places for mice, squirrels, and other small animals.

"We should continue up the trail. We seem to be leaving the tunnel. We are now back in full sun. There is milkweed growing along the trail covered in monarch butterflies. Their wings flutter from flower to flower. They look very busy. Their wings are a beautiful mixture of black, orange, and yellow with white patterns, which act as camouflage against predators. These rich and vivid colors come from layers of thousands of tiny scales. Surprisingly, butterflies don't ever eat. They have a long protruding tube called a proboscis through which they drink. They mostly drink nectar for energy. They have a wingspan of only about four inches, and butterflies never sleep. They just rest at night."

"As usual, you are a wealth of information, Memory. Here are some red cedars, and there are many red birds."

"They are cardinals, Hunter. Cardinals love red cedars and are flying all around from tree to tree. The males are brilliant red all over, with an orange bill and black face immediately around the bill. The females are mostly pale brown with reddish tinges in the wings, tail, and crest. They have the same black face and an orange bill. Cardinals are quite social and have flocks which may even include birds of other species. This trail is quite inviting. It's bustling with activity. Animals rustling in the leaves as they hear us coming, birds singing, and leaves blowing in the wind. The blooms are fragrant. It is a wonderland."

"Look to your right, Memory. There are two cottontail rabbits doing their mating ritual."

"It looks like they are fighting, Hunter."

"No, if they were fighting, they would be face-to-face swatting each other. Males fight over the females. Watch the ritual. The male will run at the female."

"Wow. The male runs to the female, and just as he arrives, she jumps high in the air and he flies under her. She hits the ground, turns around to face the male, and again jumps high in the air as he comes running at her. It actually looks like they are just playing a game. How long does this go on?"

"Not long, Memory. She has already decided to stay put so he can catch her. The serious part has begun, so let's continue on our way. To occupy your mind, I have a long list of questions for you. We should ride the horses slowly through this sparsely wooded area. First question: With your memory, how do you process and store all of that information?"

"My brain stores the stories of others in small capsules, at least that's how I think of it. Everyone I've ever met has a capsule full of details of the place, time, setting, etc. They are important to me and never forgotten. I keep them with me and sometimes open a capsule and relive the experience. One of the drawbacks of a good memory is that things get boring very quickly if only memory is used, such as playing most games. This is why I went into mathematics. I am constantly finding out new things, creating new objects in my research, being challenged, and relying on creativity. About twenty minutes is usually my limit for conversations. I easily become overstimulated by too much interaction. In a grocery store or art museum, it's necessary to go in with a game plan and get out in about twenty minutes to get away from visual, sound, scent stimuli, and other sensations. Another reason why Dorsa is a good roommate for me is that we rarely do anything together that takes more than twenty minutes."

"On no, Memory! There are two black bear cubs in a tree in front of us. Turn and get away quickly. The mother bear will be vicious if she sees us near her cubs. There is a field to our right. Let's head there."

"Hunter, contrary to popular opinion, the American black bear does not truly hibernate. Woodchucks, also called groundhogs, sleep through the entire winter and don't wake up if they are moved or hear loud noises. Bears go through 'torpor.' They wake up fairly quickly if touched or disturbed by noise. Grizzly bears can weigh eight hundred pounds and live thirty years. They are on top of the food chain and have no natural predators. Black bears are expert tree climbers because of their strong claws. Females teach their young to climb at a young age so they can climb trees to stay out of danger. Despite their waddling walk, black bears can run at twenty-five miles per hour. They are also prolific swimmers and have no trouble swimming across rivers or lakes. They have a keen sense of vision and hearing. But their best sense is smell. Their oversized noses can sniff out the tiniest morsels of food as far as a mile away."

"You are just a wealth of information, Memory. The field is covered with tall grasses, so we should walk the horses slowly through the grass. We can have lunch on the other side. Let's stop here at the end of the field and have lunch. I brought ham and cheese again. There is a hornet's nest right above us. It looks like a big blob of cotton candy. The hornets are about an inch in size and have yellow stripes which contrast with their dark bodies. They are winged and have antennae, legs, and a stinger. We will have to move."

"Hunter, hornets construct their homes from saliva and wood pulp they chew and then form into a nest. The nest consists of hexagonal combs, an outer covering, and a single entrance. The nest is only used for one year and then abandoned. Each nest is built from scratch each year."

"Interesting, Memory."

"Let's eat away from the hornet's nest, Hunter. We can tie the horses to a tree and let them eat grasses. The sandwiches are wonderful."

"Memory, what do you think about the rabbits' jumping mating ritual?"

"Looks like fun."

"Do you have a mating ritual, Memory?"

"I don't mate, Hunter. But I do know how to play leapfrog."

"Maybe we can play leapfrog one day, Memory."

"I don't think so, Hunter. That seems to be a premating ritual to you."

"Just being around you is a premating ritual to me, Memory."

"Hunter, you are straying again. You need to learn to stay on the straight and narrow."

"That sounds like a mating position to me, Memory."

"Hunter, you are once again falling off the deep end."

"That sounds like a new mating position, Memory."

"Pervert. Let's get off this topic. I see puffball and morel mushrooms I can put in my backpack. I will have to cut them open later and see if they are rotting or have bugs. There is also a stinkhorn mushroom here. It looks exactly like what was in some of the sex books my grandmother gave me."

"Memory, I think I will just let that go. We don't have to do anything about the horse manure, it will just act as fertilizer."

"Hunter, the average horse produces between fifteen and thirty-five pounds of manure a day. In the 1890s New York had a population of two hundred thousand horses producing around 2.5 million pounds of manure a day. In one year, fifteen thousand dead horses were removed from the streets. In London, this problem became known as the Great Horse Manure Crisis of 1894. The headline in the newspaper read, 'London will be seven feet deep in horse manure within 10 years.' The solution turned out to be the invention of motor transport."

"Memory, it is incredibly harmonious here. It's so relaxing. There is a stream just below us."

"Hunter, let's go down to the stream and let the horses get a drink. The water is clear. The stream is only about twelve feet wide, is shallow, and so it has a large surface area compared to its depth, which is only a couple of feet. I can see that the bottom is rock and not mud. A significant portion of the stream's nutrients falls into it from the banks which are made up of leaves, grasses, and other debris. The current's velocity is pretty fast. This influences the temperature and oxygen concentration which is much higher in a stream than in a lake. This is a beautiful stream full of life. I see crawfish wiggling around in the water and a lot of colorful minnows."

"Look over here, Memory. There is an olive-green softshell turtle. He has a flattened, pancake-like body, a long neck, and an elongated head with a snorkel-like nose. He has large webbed feet, each having three claws. We are lucky to have had a chance to see him."

"Hunter, let's skip rocks in the stream. We will have to aim down the stream. Here is a flat rock. I only managed five skips."

"Memory, I am good at this. I just got seven skips."

"Hunter, I got seven this time also. There is a cave near here we can visit. Missouri is not only the Show Me State but also the Cave

State. There are over seven thousand and five hundred known caves in Missouri. Many areas of the state are underlain by soluble carbonate bedrock, such as limestone or dolomite, that can be easily dissolved by water. Slightly acidic rainwater filters into the ground and enters cracks and joints found in the bedrock, slowly dissolving it away. In time, the groundwater enlarges these passages to form caves."

"I know about this, Memory. One of my neighbors had his tractor fall into a cave. He barely escaped alive. Let's tie off the horses. The mouth of this above-ground cave is oval and made of black rock. Let's put on our headlamps. If we are lucky, we will find Jesse James's lost hidden loot. It is cool and damp as we enter. We'll have to whisper in the cave so we don't set off a cascade of bats fleeing right at us."

"Hunter, you know I have little control over my memory. Bat excrement is called guano. It contains an exceptionally high amount of nitrogen, phosphate, and potassium. In the 1700s, it was harvested from caves to manufacture gunpowder.

"Wow, its magical in here, and the temperature is cooler than even at the entrance. The roof is covered in stalactites sticking down several feet. Their colors range from white to honey to deep red. They get their colors from organic compounds leached from soil. The floor is covered in stalagmites which are mounds sticking up from the floor formed from calcium carbonate deposited by dripping water. Careful not to step on one. There is a pool of water in front of us. We have no idea how deep it is, so we better stay back. Look how surreal our headlamps' reflections are in the pool. The water is so still. The acoustics in here are spectacular, even though we are whispering. There are echoes of breezes moving gently around the structures. Really beautiful! It's spectacular."

"I'm feeling a little claustrophobic, Memory."

"Hunter, around five to ten percent of humans are affected by severe claustrophobia. Even though the amygdala is one of the brain's smallest structures, it's also one of the most powerful. The amygdala is believed to form the core of a neural system for processing fearful and threatening stimuli. I feel it a bit also. Let's take some deep breaths and focus on the beauty of this otherworldly place. We are not in far enough for anything to fall on us."

"Thanks, that helps."

"Maybe we've enjoyed this unexplored cave enough for now. We won't have to whisper outside."

"Memory, let's take the long way home so we can talk. You must have a lot of unwanted thoughts and feelings that pop up unexpectedly from all your memories. Do you have ways of dealing with this?"

"It's amazing how frequently one of my brain's storage capsules seems to leak and sometimes at the worst times. I mostly use techniques from Aaron Beck's behavioral cognitive therapy."

"What is that?"

"The basic idea is that what we feel comes from what we are telling ourselves. There are around fifteen different distortions we can talk our way out of. For example, if we're telling ourselves something is either all good or all bad, polarization, then we can remind ourselves that most of the time things are in between these extremes."

"And that works?"

"Yes, along with deep breathing and progressive relaxation, where you tense and relax all muscle groups in your body."

"Tell me more, Memory."

"Basically the cognitive distortions are all combatted similarly. For example, fairness. If I'm telling myself something is unfair, I could experience anger, frustration, anxiety, or depression temporarily, mostly anger. Then by talking to myself, I can experience something closer to the truth of the situation. For example, tell yourself it's an anomaly and both better and worse things have happened, and you survived. This is a great help with your bantering, Hunter."

"Amazing, Memory! I'll have to try some of those techniques. What are some other distortions?"

"Filtering, always being right, overgeneralizing, blaming, shoulds, catastrophizing, jumping to conclusions, and much more. These things are only disturbing if they create a problem. People think that bad feelings like anger are caused by other people, but basically, our feelings come from what we tell ourselves. So combating negative feelings requires better self-talk. And what we tell ourselves most frequently is recorded in our brains. Sometimes in class students say, 'Sorry, that was dumb.' This is a defensive statement they are trying to make before someone else says it. I tell them to talk better to themselves. If you call yourself dumb often enough, eventually your brain will retain it as fact."

"Memory, dusk is setting in with owls, fireflies, bats, etc., all scurrying around. Everything comes to a different kind of life at dusk in the woods."

"Hunter, the sunset is gorgeous. See the deep yellows at the horizon, the rich reds above the trees as the sky fades slowly from blue to black so naturally. This glorious sunset reminds me that there is so much more to the world than just me. A gentle reminder that this too shall pass. Such a quiet, subtle, and peaceful end to a day. It is quite romantic."

"Turn on your headlamp, Memory, and point it in front of Horse so he can see where to step. Wonderful ending to a great day. We made it back to the pasture. We can put the horse tack on the back of the ATV and leave both horses here in the pasture. I assume you know that a group of horses will not all go to sleep at the same time. At least one of them will stay awake to look out for the others. Memory, you can sit on my lap on the ATV to get back to the cabin."

"Thanks, Hunter. I like sitting on your lap. I will put the horse tack under the bed. This day was an unforgettable experience. It is going to be lonely around here without Signal."

"I was hoping to stay here tonight, but I will have to get the ranch organized for my absence, so I have to go home. I will bring lunch tomorrow."

"Bye, Hunter."

Let me check the news on my new radio. The police have interviewed my grandparents, but they said they know nothing about this whole situation. The police are interviewing everyone who knows me, looking for clues to my whereabouts. The question is whether or not they have any chance of finding me.

It is lonely without Signal. I hope he is doing well. I will cook the mushrooms on the grill with butter and thyme. I can also make a grilled cheese sandwich. I have not had to eat alone in quite a while. I need to call Hunter.

"Hi, Hunter. Thanks for a great day. You continually take care of me. Thank you."

"Memory, tell me the most embarrassing moment of your life."

"Hunter, you're fading out. Can you hear me? I must be driving through a tunnel."

"Memory? Memory? She hung up. Oh, here she is. She called back."

"Sorry, Hunter. I did not want to recall that event. One time while traveling my flight was delayed eight hours. I had not slept hardly at all the night before. There was an airport hotel, so I went to the counter and asked, 'Do you rent rooms by the hour?' The airline worker said, 'Certainly not, lady. What kind of a place do you think this is?' I returned to the waiting area and explained to the women next to me what I asked, and that they refused to rent me a room. She explained to me what I had done wrong. Being homeschooled I missed that subtlety. That was really embarrassing."

"Yeah, that would be embarrassing."

"Hunter, what was your most embarrassing moment?"

"One time in college, a friend set me up with a blind date. He arranged for us to meet in front of the library at 7:00 p.m. When I arrived, this stunningly beautiful female was standing there alone. I said, 'Can I take you to dinner?' She replied, 'I would love it.' We got along pretty well until halfway through dinner I realized this was not my blind date."

"Yeah, that was embarrassing. Hunter, you never complain. But you must have problems. Everyone does."

"If I ever feel like life is unfair, I have a simple way to deal with it. I buy toys and go to the Children's Cancer Hospital. Then you see how much worse things can be and when life really is unfair. I always come away feeling lucky."

"That is really impressive. I would like to do that sometime too. I'm off to bed."

"This was a great day for me also, Memory. Sleep well."

There is Signal's ball. I hope he is doing well. Lock the shutters and door, turn on the fan, and off to bed.

14

Weird Wednesdays

I am awake. I can wash up and do my teeth. Now I will make eggs, toast, and hot coffee on the grill. This is my favorite meal. I will put the extra hot water in the thermos. It is lonely here cooking and eating alone. Hunter is already here.

"Hi, Hunter. What's the cage on the back of your ATV?"

"This is a female orphaned baby lamb. Unfortunately, twenty percent of baby lambs die before weaning. I want to save this one. She is labor intensive since she has to be bottle fed four times a day, and my ranch hands don't have the time for this. So I thought you could take care of her. Lambs are eight to twelve pounds at birth. She is ten pounds. I brought disinfectant spray since she will poop all over the cabin. Her poops have the consistency of caulking compound. I also brought four baby bottles and a combination of cow's colostrum and ewe's milk for her, some straw for a bed, and a bale of hay for her and the horses to eat. She has a collar, and here is a leash so you can walk her outside. We can make her a bed in the corner where Signal's house was. I will take the rest of the hay to the horses when I leave. Let me carry the cage inside and let her loose. I will leave the cage here with the door open and put the straw in it for her house. You spread some hay next to the cage. So you have company again.

"I cooked a pork loin and root vegetables last night. We can have it for lunch. I wrapped it heavily in foil. We need to figure out why Disk tried to kill you."

"This is a long story, Hunter, so we will have to take it in parts. It starts with my roommate in Columbia. As you know, her name is Dorsa, and we were roommates in graduate school. We hit it off instantly even though she is seven years older than me. After graduation, we both came to the University of Missouri, so it was natural for us to continue living together. In Boston, we had a furnished apartment, so in Columbia, we also rented a furnished apartment.

"We are suitable roommates. We share all bills and alternate cleaning the apartment. We both clean up after ourselves. We never touch each other's things without asking permission. Dorsa uses headphones to listen to her music so as not to disturb my doing research. We regularly go to the gymnasium to exercise together although I do martial arts class and weight machines, and Dorsa jogs on the track.

"My memory again: the name *gymnasium* derives from the Greek word *gymnos*, which means 'nude,' as all exercise and sports in ancient Greece were done by the male-only members in the nude."

"Memory, who'd a thunk it."

"We sometimes eat meals together, but otherwise do not have a lot of interaction. Most importantly, we stay out of each other's business and do not bring other people to the apartment. We never have shared our lives from before we met. I like this since I do not want people to know too much about me.

"Dorsa dated. I did not. She didn't want me to see the people she dated, but the one person I met reeked of alcohol, perfume, and was wearing jewelry. Her taste in men was none of my business. She spent a lot of time in Boonville gambling. She said she had lost money but had found a way to take care of it. This made me a little uncomfortable, but I respected her boundaries and never questioned her about it. Anyway, she must have been doing well since she always had money. Occasionally we'd have Weird Wednesdays. We'd put a sheet over the table and crawl under it. We would test each other's senses with the one being tested blindfolded. Once I had her smell limburger cheese and she said it smelled like her dad's feet. Another time she tested my sense of touch. She really had a bunch of weird feeling things. The calamari was slimy and difficult to identify, but the lobster was easy. This, of course, reminds me.

"Male lobsters' bladders are in their heads, and when they fight, they squirt each other in the face with urine."

"That's funny, Memory. I could bring a sheet and we can have Weird Wednesdays under the table."

"Don't you wish, Hunter."

"I would be happy to touch anything you will allow me to, Memory."

"Of course, you would. But it is not going to happen."

"I can give you things to touch, Memory."

"I don't think you understand the rules of the game, Hunter."

"My version doesn't have rules, Memory."

"Who do you think you are kidding, Hunter? You have been trying to get me under the sheets since you arrived."

"Memory, you know I was just bantering because the way you scrunch up your nose when frustrated makes you even more beautiful, if that is possible."

"Flattery won't get you any closer to your goal, Hunter."

"Do you blame me for trying to score a touchdown? Sorry, continue your story, Memory."

"Dorsa often went to Kansas City to see the Kansas City Royals play baseball. One time when she returned, she mentioned that there are no female players or referees in baseball.

"I said, 'While there are currently no female players in Major League Baseball, there have been in the past. The first was Lizzy Arlington, who pitched during the ninth inning for the Reading Coal Heavers in 1898 and won the game. A little over thirty years later, an African American female Jackie Mitchell pitched against the Yankees during an exhibition game. The Yankees were a major phenomenon with a lineup of both Babe Ruth and Lou Gehrig, referred to as 'murderers' row. Jackie struck out both Babe Ruth and Lou Gehrig consecutively. What's more impressive: Mitchell was only seventeen years old at the time.'

"Dorsa said, 'This is one of a long list of reasons why people call you Brain."

"Memory, let's put a kettle of water, the pork loin, and root vegetables on the grill to warm them. Continue with your story."

"One week, the university held meetings with faculty groups to discuss how to identify students who were in trouble with drugs, alcohol, in danger of suicide, or were being sex trafficked. I talked to Dorsa about the meetings we each had. I told her I found it fascinating and informative. I was impressed that the university took a very hard stance on illegal activities. They removed anyone from campus immediately even after the first violation. They removed a fraternity from campus for alcohol abuse. Their national organization then removed their charter, and the fraternity house was sold. After that, fraternities were on notice and better obeyed the rules.

"Dorsa, however, was not as happy. She said she was not impressed and said that the university clearly does not know anything about sex trafficking.

"Let's eat lunch at the picnic table. The pork loin and root vegetables are delicious. You really are quite a cook, Hunter."

"Thanks, Memory."

"Continuing my story, Dorsa and I both earn enough money to have our own apartments, but it is nice to have someone to talk to, and there is added security having two of us living in the apartment. She said her parents live in Massachusetts, so we were always apart during breaks. She has never met my grandparents, and I never told her about them. So she should not be able to find me here."

"Do you ever play games?"

"Once I learn a game, it is hard to beat me, and then I find it boring. For example, Dorsa once asked if we could play Monopoly sometime. Without telling her, I read the rules and went into the computer to do some calculations and realized that there are seven strategies which almost guarantee you will win every time. You can now find these online. I badly beat her, and she didn't want to play again. So I just showed her how to win."

"Memory, I have been using my ham radio to scan the airwaves. There is some discussion about you, but no one has any idea where you are or even if you are alive. I will drop off the hay for the horses, then I need to go to my place. I will bring a special meal for tomorrow when I come back later today."

"Bye, Hunter."

"Hi, lamb. You have beautiful short spotless snow-white wool all over. You are a little over one foot tall. Your soft furry sharp ears stick straight out from the sides of your head. You have dark rectangular pupils and a wide range of vision. You have a cute pink nose and little pink lips. Your tiny little black hoofs make quite a contrast. You are about as cute as they come, and with your ears straight out to the side and pointed nose, you remind me of a maple leaf. So I'm going to call you Maple."

I can do some sketching until Hunter comes back.

"I am back, Memory. I brought hot dogs, buns, ketchup, mustard, and marshmallows which we can have for lunch tomorrow. I also brought long-handled forks so we can cook them on an open fire. Let me put the hot dogs in the cooler."

"I named the lamb Maple. I will feed her and put some Cheerios on the floor. I am sure she will love them. Hunter, I heated the leftover pork loin and root vegetables for dinner, and we can eat at the picnic table. Great meal. It is so alive out here. Hunter, I am really down. This is all weighing on me."

"Sorry you are down, Memory. What can I do?"

"I know better than this. When we fail or make a mistake, we have a tendency to scold ourselves. It makes us feel alone in the failure. What we can do is accept that error is part of being human and talk to ourselves with care and tolerance. People often take pride in being hard on themselves, but research shows that self-criticism often backfires badly. Instead of chastising ourselves, we need to practice self-compassion and forgive our mistakes. I know all this, but because of my memory, it is often impossible to control my thoughts. And I have really bad feelings about accidentally killing Disk."

"You are the most perfect person I know, Memory. You should recall that more often."

"I certainly do not think I'm perfect, but thank you for being so supportive. I don't know what I would do without you."

"Remember, I think you are perfect. I understand that your life is a mess and you are having trouble dealing with it. But this will all be sorted out one day, and you will be able to get on with your life. It just doesn't seem like it right now. You certainly do not deserve this."

"MEMORY" SURVIVAL

"Hunter, I have all the tools to deal with this. I just need to bring them forward. Thank you for reminding me that this will be resolved one day."

"Memory, I know you disguise your memory well. Has anyone noticed much?"

"Once a fellow classmate noticed my memory and acted like my friend. Then he started blithering about various computer games he'd play and other memories of his. He started testing me in front of others about what he'd told me about the games and his memories. I managed to escape after a few incidents. It's exhausting being tested by people about their memories."

"Sounds awful, Memory. I definitely need to sleep here again tonight so you feel safe and supported. Can you go to sleep now?"

"Yes, I will take the bottom bunk. Let me set my watch alarm for midnight so I can give Maple her fourth feeding. Good night, Hunter."

"Good night, Memory."

"I don't think my alarm woke up Hunter. Up on my lap, Maple. You really love being fed. Down you go, and I am back to bed."

"Oh no. I just woke up and am in trouble. Hunter, get up. Hunter, get up quickly. I am having an angioedema attack. Get an EpiPen off the shelf."

"I'll just jump off the top bunk and run to the shelf."

"The EpiPens are preloaded injections in individual boxes. Bring one here. Stick it in my outer thigh right through my pants and inject the epinephrine."

"Memory, you have huge swollen red blotches on your forehead, lips, cheeks, arms, and ears. It looks frightening."

"And my trachea is starting to swell shut. The epinephrine should work quickly."

"Is there anything I can do?"

"Hunter, there is nothing more you can do but wait. When people are faced with a stressful situation, there is a release of adrenaline. This helps you focus so you can face the danger. When the stress goes away, you stop producing adrenaline. I produce much more adrenaline than most people, especially when I am stressed, and

I may produce excessive amounts for hours. When it finally stops, I go into adrenaline withdrawal, leading to angioedema. At least that is how I think of it. The stress of my situation is catching up to me."

"Memory, the blotches are going down. That was very scary."

"I am used to it. I should take my antihistamine medication, diphenhydramine. It's on the shelf."

"Memory, here is a cup of water and two pills."

"I will be all right now, but we are both upset and won't be able to sleep."

"Memory, you have once again scared me to death. This is so frightful, I will not be able to sleep at the ranch anymore for worrying about you."

"Hunter, you can stay here at night if you want to. Normally my life is incredibly routine: teach, do research, exercise, etcetera, but this crazy circumstance has turned my life upside down."

"Memory, having you call me every night helps but does not solve the problem."

"Hunter, I don't know what to do. I am just trying to survive."

"I want to make sure that you do survive for my sake as well as yours."

"I think we can go back to sleep now. Good night, Hunter."

"Good night, Memory."

15

Dying by Suicide

"Good morning, Hunter. I am really having difficulty getting things off my mind so I can sleep. I constantly wake up during the night. The problem is not just my situation. Maple kept me up most of the night clippity-clopping all around the cabin. She only slept four hours. She talked all night with her little baas—high and low tones, calm and stressed. Also, the coyotes were howling with their high-pitched barks and yips. Adding to this, the whip-poor-wills, screech owls, and a great horned owl hooting, it's impossible to sleep."

"Sheep only sleep four hours a night, Memory. It was like an out-of-tune Philharmonic Orchestra here last night. We definitely need earplugs."

"Maple, time for breakfast. Get up here on my lap and take your milk. Now you can run around. Hunter, grab two oranges, and I will make eggs, toast, and coffee on the grill. We can eat outside."

"This is a nice meal, Memory. We should continue with your story, but first, tell me something I do not know."

"In the wild, hamsters are alcoholic animals. They hoard ryegrass seeds and fruit in their burrows, and they eat this fermenting store as it becomes more and more alcoholic over the winter. Hamsters don't just tolerate alcohol. When in captivity, they prefer it to water. That might be because they're drinking for the calories. If a human drank as much alcohol as a hamster in one sitting, you would die."

"Well, I definitely did not know that. Let's get to your story, Memory."

"I had a student named Jade in my computer engineering course. She was exceptional—was always in class, did her homework perfectly, and had the highest scores on her tests. Then all of a sudden, it fell apart. She started skipping class, often did not get her homework done, and her grades were slipping. So I called her into my office to see what was going on. She said that her parents were getting divorced, and it was really upsetting her. She would try to get her life back together. I set her up an appointment with counseling services.

"Things did not improve, so I called her back into my office. I was worried she might be on drugs or alcohol. As it turns out, she did not go to counseling services. She swore she was not on drugs or alcohol. This time, I demanded she go, or I would have to report her to the dean's office. She was on a scholarship, and this requires that we report when a scholarship student might be violating the terms of their scholarship. This time she went to counseling services.

"But still no improvement. Now I realized from my meeting with the university on students in peril that she might be sex trafficked. She had some of the signs: academically unengaged, performs under grade level, sudden change in academic performance, appears malnourished, gaps in memory, and low self-esteem. So for a third time, I called her into my office. I was also worried she could be suicidal, so this time, I took her to the counseling center and checked her in. I assumed they would take care of the problem.

"A week later, she died by suicide from a massive overdose of ibuprofen and alcohol. Today, we no longer say that someone 'committed suicide' but instead say they 'died by suicide.' I immediately went to counseling services to find out what went wrong, but they were not allowed to talk to me. I wanted to contact her parents, but there are strict federal laws guaranteeing confidentiality of students—even from their parents. But I could not let this go.

"I started to search her records. I did not find anything unusual, except that she had been picked up three times by campus security for being in trouble. Once, a bar downtown called campus security and told them to come get her or they would call the city police. Another time, she was passed out on the campus lawn. I entered her website and found sexually explicit material, which is one sign of being sex trafficked.

"Now I really could not let this go, but I was not sure what I could do. I mentioned my concerns to Dorsa, but she said, 'I don't believe sex trafficking could happen on campus. The university is on top of almost everything going on here. It is more likely that this student was into prostitution on her own.' She was right in that this may not be on campus but rather someone might just be recruiting on campus. If you are looking for vulnerable females, the campus is the place to come.

"Still, I was concerned and had to look into it. I spent two hours a night scouring the internet for information. Along the way, I came across an escort website. I never knew this existed locally, and I was immediately uncomfortable since these sites are often disguises for prostitution. There was no information whatsoever about who owned the website or who the escorts were. The IP address was the public library.

"I decided to check into the webpages of female students, which was no minor feat since we have around 16,000 female students. Finally, I came up with six names that I thought might fit the criteria for being sex trafficked. Next, I went through their university records and discovered that all of them had been picked up by campus security at various times for alcohol-related offenses. I then went through all the campus police reports and discovered that all six had been picked up by one campus police officer: Disk Banks. This stood out like a sore thumb. I again talked to Dorsa and said maybe I should go to the university. She said, 'That is not a good idea. You don't have any concrete evidence of anything, and you could cause a mess and get someone in trouble for no reason.' I agreed that I should not get involved in such serious accusations without concrete evidence.

"I knew Disk since, as an MU alumnus, I volunteered with the alumni association to help plan Homecoming Weekend, which is in October. But it is a very complicated event and needs quite a bit of organization. It includes a blood drive, a talent competition, decorating downtown, campus decorations, a homecoming parade on campus and downtown, with floats and sometimes includes the Budweiser Clydesdales. The main event is the homecoming football game. The head of campus security, Birch, was at the meeting, along with Disk Banks.

"This, of course, reminds me. In 1891 the Missouri Tigers faced off against the Kansas Jayhawks in the first installment of the 'border war,' the oldest football rivalry west of the Mississippi River. This intense rivalry originally took place at neutral sites, usually in Kansas City. The NCAA was founded in 1906 to regulate the rules of college sport and protect young athletes, since at that time college football was known as a very brutal sport. They introduced a new conference regulation requiring intercollegiate football games be played on collegiate campuses. To renew excitement in the rivalry, ensure adequate attendance at the new location, and celebrate the first meeting of the two teams on the Mizzou campus in Columbia, Mizzou athletic director Chester Brewer invited all alumni to 'come home' for the game in 1911. It was centered on a parade, and the response was so great it became an annual event eventually known as homecoming, which then spread across the US."

"Memory, I graduated from MU but did not know that MU started the tradition of homecoming. We should break for lunch. I will make a fire in the firepit so we can cook the hot dogs and marshmallows. In the meantime, we can go give Horse and Bolt some carrots. This walk to the pasture is becoming second nature even for me. Are there beavers around here?"

"There are many beavers in Missouri, Hunter, but they do not commonly build dams as they do in other parts of the country. I have seen their tracks near the creek, but I have never seen a beaver. Beavers have translucent eyelids so they can see while swimming underwater. They also have orange teeth. Other rodents have magnesium in their tooth enamel which makes their teeth white, but beavers have iron, which makes their teeth orange and stronger for chomping wood. Iron is also what makes our blood red."

"Interesting, Memory! Here are some carrots, Horse and Bolt."

"Hunter, save some carrots."

"MEMORY" SURVIVAL

"Horses, we will ride you again sometime. Memory, we can run our fingers under the horses' manes, rub their sides and noses, and stroke their ears. We should feel their legs to make sure there are no problems or swelling."

"Hunter, you may not know that horses disappeared from the Americas more than eleven thousand years ago. They don't know why. Every horse in the US is a decedent of European horses brought here in the 1500s by the Spanish explorers. Even the horses that we regard as wild are actually feral horses, whose ancestors escaped from captivity."

On the way home I want to try something. Let me shout, "Signal, want some carrots? Signal, want some carrots? Wow, here he comes a running. He certainly loves his carrots. Great to see you again, Signal. Here are some carrots. I miss you.

"Hunter, the fire should be ready. Let's walk back to the cabin. I have not had a cookout like this since I was young. I will put the hot dogs, buns, mustard, ketchup, and marshmallows on the table, and you get the utensils and the skewers. It is actually fun holding the hot dogs over the fire and spinning them to get an even blistering. Tasty."

"Memory, we should listen to the radio. Oh no. Foster Brandon of the agriculture department has been found dead in his apartment. When he did not show up for work, they sent the campus police to look for him. They don't have a cause of death yet, so they do not know if it is suspicious. I knew him since I took two courses from him."

"Hunter, I knew him well since I have a research grant with him. This is unbelievable. He was fine the last time I saw him."

"This is unnerving. We should keep up with this on the radio. At least this has knocked you out of the news. For now, let's roast marshmallows over the coals."

"Hunter, I need to replace some of the shakes on the roof. Can you get me thirty shakes, a ladder, chisel, hammer, and nails, please."

"Yes, I will bring them tonight. I need to go and work on the books for the ranch, pay the ranch hands, and the mortgage."

"Hunter, you probably don't know that the word *mortgage* comes from the old French word *mort*, which meant 'dead,' and *gage*, which meant 'pledge.' So when you take out a mortgage you are literally making a 'dead pledge.'"

"Memory, I certainly did not know that. But I did know about the expression 'He bought the farm,' meaning he died and his life insurance paid off the farm. I will come back tonight and bring the stuff for the roof, and some earplugs. I do not want you up on the roof alone, so I will stay tomorrow and help you with the repairs."

"Hunter, I have a bag of trash here, can you take it and dispose of it, please?"

"Your wish is my command."

"I am speechless. No one has ever said something so kind to me before. Bye, Hunter. See you later."

Now I have to keep myself busy this afternoon. I will take Maple for a walk down to the pasture. Let me put on her leash, head outside, and put the leaf in the door.

"I am not sure it is safe for you to be around horses, Maple, so I cannot let you into the pasture. We will just walk back to the cabin."

I'll put BenGay on my forehead and go from thing to thing today. One hour on my piano at the table. Now one hour sketching, followed by one hour doing martial arts. I wish I could concentrate well enough to do my research, but it is just not possible at this moment because of the latest news. Also, Maple playing with the ball is distracting. That really used up the time.

Hunter is here.

"Memory, I brought earplugs, two large potatoes, the shakes, a ladder, my toolbox, rope, and roofing nails made of hot-dipped galvanized steel which are best for shakes."

"Hunter, let's grill ham and cheese sandwiches and the potatoes in foil. I will stab the potatoes with a fork so they do not explode. We can practice sign language while the potatoes cook."

"You are getting really good at sign language, Memory. Not surprising, given your IQ."

"Hunter, let me feed Maple. You grill the sandwiches. Time to eat, Maple. You just did a binky. Good girl. Up on my lap. Try not to keep us up all night. Thanks for listening to my story, Hunter. I needed to tell it to someone. We can eat."

"MEMORY" SURVIVAL

"You are very welcome, Memory. I am all ears around you."

"No bantering today, Hunter. Have you lost your touch?"

"Was that a pun, Memory?"

"You know full well that I did not mean 'touch' in that way, Hunter."

"I am just trying to get to first base, Memory."

"You won't get off home plate, Hunter."

"Maybe I could play first base and field you, Memory."

"Well, you dropped the ball, Hunter."

"So no chance of me hitting a home run, Memory?"

"Not today, Hunter. You have used up your bantering allowance for the day. Nice meal, Hunter. The cabin is hot. We may have trouble sleeping in this heat. Let's keep the shutters open. Also, the fan will help. I'm tired enough that I can probably go to sleep, and I am much more relaxed when you are here. Thanks for staying. Good night, Hunter."

"Put in your earplugs, Memory. Good night."

16

The Fugitive

I woke up tired since the uncertainty of my situation is constantly weighing on me. I need to fill two of Maple's milk bottles.

"Maple, what are you doing on the table? You could get hurt. Get on my lap and take your milk. Good girl. Hunter is still sleeping.

"Get up, Hunter. Today is a good day for pancakes, maple syrup, and hot coffee. The water is already hot on the grill, and the rest of the stuff is on the picnic table. I will go start the pancakes and make us a cup of coffee."

"These pancakes are good, Memory. I slept really deeply last night, knowing you were safe."

"Hunter, can Maple be around the horses?"

"Yes, she can. I need to go to the ranch and get the new list of stuff you need. It will just take an hour."

"Bye, Hunter."

I need to keep busy for an hour. Let me listen to the radio. This is not good. I will have to tell Hunter. Let me do a good cleaning of Maple's poops and the floor. I hear Hunter already.

"I'm back, Memory. I brought another cooler with ice, eggs, milk, more milk for Maple, lunch meats, and cheese. I also brought canned ham, a loaf of bread, flour, baking powder, cocoa powder, granulated sugar, vanilla, and a six pack of Coca-Cola."

"Hunter, the name Coca-Cola derives from the fact that the original formula contained cocaine. It was invented in 1885 by John

"MEMORY" SURVIVAL

Pemberton, a pharmacist from Georgia. At that time, cocaine was legal and was often used in medicine. The name *cola* comes from the cocaine in an extract of the cocoa leaf, and *cola* comes from the Kola nut, which was also an ingredient. Eventually, cocaine had to be removed from the formula since it became illegal."

"I certainly did not know that, Memory. I will take the cooler inside, and you can grab the rest of the items. Hi, Maple. You seem to be doing fine. Moving around constantly is good, it will strengthen your legs. I need to hear more of your story Memory, but we should first fix the roof before it gets too hot. The pounding on the roof will be too much for Maple. So I will take her to the pasture and let her play with the horses. In the meantime, you put up the ladder and leave the other stuff next to it.

"Let me put on your leash, Maple, and let's go to the pasture. This is a fun walk, even for you. Here we are. You can go play, and I will go back to the cabin.

"Memory, I'm back. I will go up on the roof and bring one end of the rope with me. You can tie fifteen of the shakes in a bundle, and I will lift the shakes up and then throw one end of the rope back down for another bundle. That works. Now tie the rope to the handle of my toolbox so I can lift it up to the roof while you climb up.

"In the toolbox are two hammers, two chisels, and two boxes of nails. We need to chisel the bad shakes into smaller pieces and pull them out. Then use the claw of the hammer to pull out the nails and put them in the toolbox. Since we are pulling shakes out of the middle of the roof, we need to lift the shake above it a little and push the new shake under it. We will not be able to nail it at the top. Just nail it wherever you can. We can burn the old shakes in the firepit since they are just untreated cedar."

"I am hot, Hunter."

"Memory, you just fulfilled my wildest dream."

"I meant temperature-wise, Hunter."

"At least that is a start, Memory."

"A start towards what, Hunter?"

"Towards your ultimate happiness, Memory."

"That is your ultimate happiness, Hunter. Not mine."

"Memory, I once read that 'happiness is doing naughty things together.'"

"I believe you wrote that, Hunter."

"We could get undressed and jump in the creek, Memory."

"Why do I believe that if I ever took my clothes off, you would not be jumping in the creek, Hunter?"

"But I would be drowning over you, Memory."

"You're already 'all wet', Hunter."

"Memory, it only took two hours to install the new shakes, which is good since it is getting very hot. You get off the roof, and I will use the rope to lower the toolbox. We can put my toolbox under the bed. That is one thing about log cabin living. Space is at a premium. We did a good job. We work well together. Let's cool off in the creek."

"After our discussion on the roof, I am not going anywhere near the creek with you, Hunter. You go grab Maple. I will prepare lunch. I can make sandwiches of lunch meat and cheese that you brought."

"I'm off. Back soon."

Hunter has been gone quite a while.

"Hunter, what took so long?"

"Maple was determined not to be caught, so I had to chase her all over the pasture. As a consequence, I got stung by a bee."

"If you have a reaction, as you know, I have EpiPens. The only bees that might sting you are females. They have two sets of chromosomes like us. The queen is the only female in the hive that is fertile. Males, called drones, have a single set of chromosomes from the queen. They literally do not have a father. How is it that the queen manages to lay two sorts of eggs? The answer is absolutely ingenious. When the drones mate with the queen, she stores their sperm in a special organ called the spermatheca. This sits conveniently alongside the tube through which her eggs are passed. Depending upon how she squeezes this organ, she decides which eggs will be female and which will be male. It's an incredible system in which the mother can choose the sex of her offspring to meet the conditions. The drone's only function is to mate with the queen and then die. The females then eat them. What a strange hierarchy."

"As usual, you are a wealth of information, Memory."

"Hi, Maple. It is time for your lunch. It just takes a few minutes. See how she just sits on my lap, Hunter. She loves the bottle. I can wash out the bottles in the basin. Let's eat the sandwiches outside. Are we ready for the rest of my story?"

"Go for it."

"I was now quite suspicious about Disk Banks, so I started looking into his background. He attended the Law Enforcement Training Institute (LETI) here at MU. They offer a class A-certified 600-hour basic training academy. That's a progressive and fast-paced academy. The moment you punch the clock on day 1, you are assigned a squad, squad leader, and chain of command. You are treated like an officer, and you are expected to act like one. Our police faculty is one of the most distinguished and widely recognized groups of professionals in law enforcement training. Recruits and veteran officers from all fifty states and Canada graduate from their training programs.

"After graduating, Disk took a job in the police department in Chicago, where he was for several years. Next, he applied to come back to MU to be a campus police officer. Since it can be difficult transitioning from a large-city police department to the much-different atmosphere of a campus police department, he was put on probation under Birch, the head of campus security. We currently have forty-nine campus police.

"I was convinced Disk was up to no good, but there was nothing in any university records negative about him. I searched the internet for information, but he had no webpage, and I found no other information. Since he had picked up several students on Friday and Saturday nights, I decided to follow him to see what he was up to. I tried to be very discreet. He made contact with several of the students I suspected of being sex trafficked, so I was convinced he was running a sex trafficking ring on campus. Finals were just starting, so I had to postpone my work on this. Eventually, I went back to investigating Disk. Finally, I told Dorsa one Saturday night that I was going to the university Monday morning to report him. Then as I told you, Monday morning Dorsa went to work early, and Disk showed up at my apartment to kill me. He apparently figured out that I was following him. That is all I know.

"Hunter, this morning I heard on the radio that the coroner said Foster Brandon died of a broken neck. It does not look like an accident, and they found a martial arts pin clasped in his hand. This definitely points in my direction again. But anybody can buy a martial arts pin online. So now I am a person of interest in two murders. I certainly did not do it. Someone is trying to frame me for murder. But why? What a catastrophe. They are searching for me by helicopter, but there are hundreds of square miles to search, and they do not know what they are looking for."

"Memory, this makes your situation even more confusing. It looks like some group tried to kill you, and when they failed, they decided to frame you for murder. But what is their motivation?

"I hear a helicopter in the distance. They could be looking for you. If they see the horses, it will give you away. Quick, grab the bridles. We must get to the pasture fast and bring the horses under the oak trees. Run. Open the gate, grab Horse, and I'll grab Bolt. Ride fast to the cabin, and we will tie them under the oak trees. Help me carry the gas grill into the cabin. We seem to have beaten the helicopter. It's now overhead. It's just flying by, but let's leave the horses here for a while. That was scary.

"To get our minds off this, tell me what it's like traveling and lecturing."

"What I have discovered over time traveling in other countries is that people everywhere are basically the same. They are living under the radar, just trying to survive, and everyone is special in some way. Every place I go I enjoy meeting people in coffee shops, parks, airports, buses, trams, trains, in classes, at meetings, at dinners, etc. If you take the time to interact with strangers, you gain a lot of perspective. When in a foreign country, sometimes the easiest way to get started learning a foreign language is to get a children's picture dictionary and go over it with a child. There are always children around."

"Memory, let me take the horses back to the pasture."

"I'm back, Memory. Tell me more about how your memory works."

"Since people change opinions, behaviors, and personalities occasionally, my memory capsules update but retain the originals since the change might be temporary. My memories come whole or in pictures out of thin air. When asked about something, my memory might go rapidly and automatically through the alphabet one letter at a time until the memory pops out. I always thought my brain did that because my father taught me to alphabetize at age two so I could put his students' names in order. My mind moves very rapidly, so I am constantly changing topics. This confuses many people since they are often responding to something I said several topics ago, but I'd already moved on. That must be irritating for them."

"Oh no, Memory. There are two policemen with guns outside. You stay here and keep Maple quiet. Let me open the door and go out."

"Hello, gentlemen. What can I do for you?"

"Do you own this cabin?"

"Yes."

"Why are you here?"

"I own a two thousand-acre ranch just west of here. I grow wheat and have five thousand sheep. The coyotes have been killing my sheep, so I have been hunting them here."

"We are from the Boone County Sheriff's Department and are looking for a fugitive named Coral Holmes. Our helicopter saw this cabin, and it is not on the map, so we parked south of here and walked in to check it out. Have you seen this person?"

"The cabin is not on the map since this property is part of my ranch, and my parents built the cabin years ago. I have been coming here every day for three weeks and have not seen anyone during that time. But if I do, I will call you."

If these guys see the horses, it will make them suspicious why I have an ATV and two horses. I can try to claim someone else is storing their horses here, but they may still be suspicious. So I need to steer them away from the pasture, which is west of the cabin.

"Coral Holmes is not here, so you might as well walk back south to your car."

"Thank you. Have a good day."

"Good luck with your search."

"Memory, that was a close one. For sure I need to stay here tonight just in case they come back."

"That's fine, Hunter. I like it when you stay here."

"We need to keep our ears open for helicopters, and if we hear one, we need to grab the horses in a hurry and bring them up here again. There is little time left in the day. Can you tell me about some of your mathematics?"

"This is difficult since it requires a long list of definitions, but I have a talk, Mathematical Insanity, which is a collection of completely surprising and amazing applications to the real world of elementary mathematics. I give this talk to high school math clubs, and it doesn't require any real knowledge of mathematics."

"Sounds great."

"To start, the average sheet of paper is .007 inches thick. Suppose I take the paper and fold it in half, then fold it in half again, then continue to fold it in half fifty-one times. How high is my stack of paper? Is it as high as this table? As high as the cabin? Actually, it is 106,319,609 miles high and has passed the sun in our solar system."

"Amazing. Do you have more?"

"Suppose I make a box a thousand and a hundred yards on a side. This is eleven football fields laid end to end for the length, width, and height. This box would fit inside the city of Columbia. But this is a really large box. It contains almost thirty-six billion cubic feet. This box is so big every man, woman, and child on earth would fit inside of it right in the middle of the city of Columbia."

"Unbelievable, Memory."

"Another. A *billion* was a word not known by the average citizen one hundred years ago. Now, the US government spends $1 billion every 6 hours. But this is really a large number."

1) "Suppose you invested $1 billion in a bad company which loses $1,000 a day, seven days a week, week after week, and year after year. You may worry if your children will have any inheritance. But no worries. Even at this rate it

"MEMORY" SURVIVAL

will take the company three thousand years to lose your investment.

2) If I magnify the cap of my pen one billion times, it will now be ninety-five thousand miles long and eight thousand miles wide, and the entire earth would fit inside it.
3) A billion is so large that it was not until 10:40 a.m. on April 20, 1902, that a billion minutes had elapsed since the beginning of our calendar two thousand years ago.
4) You might hope $1 billion in $1 bills is scattered in a field. You and your friends could bring pickup trucks and collect it. But this will do no good. A billion dollars in $1 bills weighs a thousand tons, and it would take a freight train to carry it away.
5) Now that we have decided a billion is a truly large number, it may actually not be that large since there are more than 1 billion ways to receive change for a $5 bill."

"You are just a wealth of incredible information, Memory."

"Hunter, we'd better have a cold meal since we don't want to cook outside with the sheriff's men around. You make sandwiches, and we can have a cold can of green beans. I will feed Maple. Maple, time for dinner. I will give you your bottle while you are standing up."

"Memory, don't all of those memories ever get all tangled up somehow?"

"Yes, and it's awful. It's a very good thing I was able to complete my testing for degrees at a very young age. The more I read, learn, and experience, the more difficulties with storing information in isolated brain capsules. Eventually, taking tests would have become intolerable and nearly impossible unless they were given in person orally in short bursts.

"Thanks for the sandwiches, Hunter. I guess it is off to bed for both of us. Sleep well."

"As long as I dream about you. I sleep great. Good night, Memory."

I can't sleep! Get up and turn on the lantern. Attack of the leaking memory capsules. My life will never be the same. I need to get out of here. What am I going to do? Stop it! Think in terms of percentages to stop catastrophizing. What are the chances I'll be fired? Nearly zero since I am innocent. What are the odds I'll be stuck here forever? Nearly zero. What is the probability I'm in danger here from someone? Slightly more than zero.

I need to find something to keep busy. I guess I can draw again. That is working. Maple is confused by the lantern and my being up. I might as well feed her. At least I did not wake up Hunter. I will try going back to bed now.

17

Swollen Up

Last night was tough. I need to feed Maple. First fill her two bottles.

"On my lap, kid. You enjoy this interaction, don't you?"

I need to clean up after Maple. Hunter brought plenty of paper towels and disinfectant spray. Dump this stuff in a trash bag. Hunter is up.

"Good morning, sleepyhead. How did you sleep last night?"

"Great. Being around you so I know you are safe relaxes me."

"Hunter, let's take the grill outside. I'll make eggs, toast, and put the kettle on. You set up the picnic table."

"At least the sheriff's men did not return. I feel we are in great danger of being found, but there's nothing we can do about it."

"Breakfast is ready, Hunter."

"Tastes great, Memory. I will have to go back to my place and the store again. It should only take an hour. I may have to consider opening a grocery delivery service."

"Are you saying I'm high maintenance?"

"Not compared to Maple, Memory."

"Now are you comparing me to a lamb?"

"Not unless you start sitting on my lap to eat."

"That could be fun. Say goodbye, Hunter."

I can draw a couple sketches while he's gone. I hear his ATV.

"Hunter, your right leg is covered in blood. What happened?"

"I was upset about something and was not paying close enough attention to what I was doing, so I did not see the razorback hog next to the path. He charged at my ATV and gored me in the thigh."

"There's a lot of blood, Hunter. At least the tusks have missed your femoral artery. This is serious. Put your arm around my shoulder, and I will help you into the cabin. As you know, my memory doesn't quit even in an emergency.

"Razorbacks have been known to attack without provocation and have killed humans. They were introduced in North America by the Spanish explorers. Males have sharp, tusks which can really slice you up. They are more common in Arkansas. Since 1910, the University of Arkansas has used the razorback as its mascot after football coach Hugo Bezdek proclaimed the team played like a 'wild band of razorback hogs.'

"Let's get you set down on the bed. Give me your belt, and take off your pants."

"Thanks, Memory. I thought you'd never ask."

"You just can't help yourself even in pain. I will have to put a tourniquet just above the wound. If this does not completely stop the bleeding, I will have to put another four inches above that one."

"This could be fun. I may need a third tourniquet above those."

"You just can't get your mind off that topic, can you, Hunter?"

"Ouch! That really hurts, Memory! Give me a cup of that whiskey. At least that's what they do in cowboy movies."

"Hunter, isn't it a bit early in the morning for whiskey?"

"Then put a Cheerio in it."

"They also say 'Cowboy up' in cowboy movies, which you are going to have to do to get through this. Here's some aspirin and a cup of water. I need to work on these wounds. It will be hands on. You better not get aroused."

"You mean I'm not?"

"You don't know?"

"Guess I didn't realize that it was just my leg that was swollen."

"You're incorrigible, Hunter. I have stopped the bleeding and put on some antibiotic ointment. These wounds need pressure to keep the bleeding stopped. I will put gauze on them and duct-tape it tightly. I can remove the tourniquet. You better just lie on the bed for now. I'll soak your pants in water. Here's a pair of your jogging pants you brought me. Luckily you were hit with tusks and not bitten, or you would have to go to the hospital and be checked for rabies. But keep in mind that medical errors may be the sixth leading cause of death in the US."

"Memory, sometimes your memory can be really scary. I wish I did not know now what I did not know then. Get my gun and box of bullets out of the ATV. I still bring it every day in case we need it. I bought eight cooked pork chops at the supermarket. I also brought sandwiches, potato salad, canned beans, another canned ham, Maple's milk, a large jar of instant coffee, ice, and a game called Sequence. This game might work for you since the outcome is determined by the luck of the draw of the cards. Also, to be safe, move my ATV behind the cabin."

I will go out and get the gun and bullets and put them on an upper shelf. Next, I will get the rest of the stuff. I need to empty the water from the coolers, but they are heavy. I'll just drag them to the edge of the porch and pull out the plug at the bottom so the water drains out. Two such trips was work. Now I can add the new ice, the rest of the stuff, and put the ATV behind the cabin.

"How did the razorback surprise you?"

"When I got home, the police were at my house, and as soon as I saw the police car in the driveway, I panicked. As it turned out, they were inquiring about Foster Brandon. I explained that I knew nothing. Luckily, they seem to have forgotten all about you with this new murder to deal with. But on the way here, this interaction was on my mind, and I was not paying enough attention. So the razorback startled me."

"At least you did not sit on him, or we would be reliving an old scenario. We can have your sandwiches and potato salad for lunch. You can have yours sitting up in bed."

"Thanks, Memory. This is good."

"Just take a nap to start the recovery process. While you are sleeping, I will make a German chocolate cake. Surprisingly, the cake is not from Germany. It was invented by an American baker by the name of Samuel German, so it was originally called German's chocolate cake. A cake will really test my cooking skills with this wood stove. Let me put the cake in the oven."

Hunter seems to be in a fever dream. "Memory, I love you."

Is that him or the fever talking?

"Memory, marry me. I love you."

He must really be in a fever dream. I wonder if he even knows what he is saying. He has passed out, which is probably good. He should sleep all afternoon. I'll put a wet towel on his forehead. I don't think it will wake him. I need to feed Maple.

"Maple, up on my lap. You are growing fast."

I better listen to the radio with earphones to hear what is going on with my case. The police don't have any new clues, but they are thoroughly convinced I am still alive, and am the main person of interest in two murders. There is an all-out search for me.

I need to keep busy this afternoon. I will make sketches. Hunter has made me think about my life. I've never had a close friend. My whole life has been alone doing my research, traveling, and lecturing. I have never had anyone to share my life or thoughts with. Being with Hunter has introduced me to a different lifestyle. Having someone to share my time, thoughts, feelings, joys, and fears with is much more fulfilling then just doing research. Maybe there should be more to life than just my career.

Is Hunter offering me a partnership for a future life? Could I come home to him every day after work and share my day with him? Would he stop bantering, or is it part of his psyche? Would I even want him to? I think I'm already finding it fun and challenging.

Hunter is awake.

"You're awake, Hunter. You had fever dreams and were talking. Do you remember what you said?"

"I don't remember anything. I hope I was at least polite. What did I say?"

"You were talking about your future. Looks like you know what you want."

"Memory, I need to go to the outhouse."

"Are you sure you can make it?"

"MEMORY" SURVIVAL

"Either that, or I poop in the corner like Signal used to."

"Take my grandfather's walking stick and lean on me. It will be a slow slog to the outhouse. I will wait out here. Put a scoop of lime in the hole when you are done."

"Thanks, Memory."

"Now back to the cabin, Hunter. You better rest in bed. Finally, I get to take care of you. I need to make us dinner. Will you be okay if I warm up some pork chops on the grill? We can have potato salad with it."

"I will be fine with Maple keeping me company."

I have four pork chops in foil on the grill. We will have four pork chops left.

While it is heating, I can set the table and feed Maple.

"Hunter, sit on the edge of the bed, and I will give you your plate and buttered bread. I will eat at the table. We have cake for dessert."

"Tastes great, Memory. The cake is wonderful. Thank you and thank you for taking care of me."

"Let me clean up. You rest. You will have to sleep here tonight. I will sleep on the top bunk. If you need anything, wake me."

"See you in the morning, Memory."

"See you in the morning, Hunter. Sleep well."

18

The Toothbrush Fairy

Hunter seems to have slept through the night, but he is going to feel bad this morning. I will get some water and a couple of ham slices heating on the grill.

"Maple, time for breakfast. You now know what that means and come running. I think you also like me holding you on my lap. Now try not to make too much noise and wake Hunter. Actually, it doesn't matter since I see him sitting up."

"Memory has a little lamb, a little lamb, a little lamb. Memory has a little lamb, its fleece is white as snow."

"Are you delusional again?"

"I am always delusional around you, Memory."

"I know that, Hunter, but are you okay?"

"As okay as possible."

"Here's a mug of coffee. We can have cake for breakfast. I also grilled some ham to build up your strength. Can you make it to the table?"

"I am moving as I speak, even if very slowly. Get out from under my feet, Maple. This is great, thank you. Memory, tell me something I don't know."

"Contrary to popular opinion, the color red doesn't make bulls angry. Bulls are color-blind."

"I'll need to use your toothbrush."

"Go for it."

"Memory, we have never even kissed, but we are already exchanging bodily fluids. What does that mean?"

"It means your mind is going loopy again. Only you could turn a toothbrush into a sexual object."

"This is more than a kiss. It is like a kiss with tongue, Memory."

"I am almost afraid to give you the toothpaste."

"It is a lubricant, after all."

"For your teeth, Hunter. Do you need dental floss?"

"I think of dental floss as a thong for your teeth."

"Pervert. Who do you think you are? The toothbrush fairy? I don't think I will ever be able to brush again without those images. You know, you do not have to express every perverted thought in your head."

"But frustration enhances your natural beauty, Memory."

"You've used up your perversion allotment for today. Let me clean up, and you go lie on the bed. I don't think you should be moving around too much today. I don't want you to open your wounds."

"Memory, tell me something else I don't know."

"Spider silk is stronger than steel. The material is light and flexible, and a strand of steel of the same thickness is weaker than a strand of silk."

"I certainly didn't know that."

"Now you tell me something I don't know, Hunter."

"I don't know much about anything besides agriculture. Something interesting about sheep is that they have no upper front teeth. Instead, their lower teeth press against a hard upper pallet to chew."

"I didn't know that."

"Maybe I'll take a nap."

While Hunter is sleeping, I can do some sketches. I will play my paper piano for a while. Oh no! I made a mistake. Now I have to start all over again. Hunter's being injured has seriously upset me. That is enough.

"Maple, it is time for lunch. I will feed you while you are standing next to me. You really are high maintenance, as Hunter said."

Hunter is up.

"Hunter, we should have sandwiches and potato salad for lunch."

"Potato salad is one of my favorites."

"Who could have guessed? Get to the table, your lunch is on a plate."

"I do feel a little better now."

"I'm glad."

"Let's practice sign language this afternoon, Memory."

"Sounds good."

"Memory, tell me what I just signed."

"You said, 'It is nice knowing you.'"

"Great. Now you sign me. Very good. You said, 'You are a good friend.' Now let me give you another."

"Hunter, did you say you want to have sex? Can't you even control yourself while signing?"

"Memory, actually, I said I want to go home. These signs are close. For *sex*, the bent index finger is first placed on the right jawline and then the right temple. For *home*, your right fingertips touch the side of your mouth and then your ear. Now you try again. Nice job. You said, 'The weather is good today'. Now sign a second time. You said, 'I go out menstruating'. Did you mean that?"

"Hunter, I said, 'I go out daily.' I think you are twisting what I am saying to fit your bantering needs."

"Memory, I wouldn't do that. This is too serious. Those two signs are close to each other. One taps the cheek twice with the closed fist, and the other slides down the cheek twice with the closed fist. You are very good at sign language. We should practice again sometime.

"Let's play Sequence at the table. We each get a bag of chips and seven cards from the double deck. The board has two pictures of each of the playing cards except the jacks. If you have a card in your hand, you can put a chip on that card on the board. Then discard the card and pick a new one from the deck. If you get five chips in a row horizontally, vertically, or diagonally, you have a sequence. Two sequences wins the game. Two-eyed jacks are wild and allows you to put a chip anywhere while one-eyed jacks allow you to take one of my pieces off the board. Jokers go in the four corners and can be used by both players."

"Okay, Hunter. Here is my first play."

"MEMORY" SURVIVAL

"We continue to alternate."

"Memory, somehow you got a sequence quite quickly. That is unusual. And now you have four chips in a row. I will use a one-eyed jack to remove one of these chips before you get another sequence."

"That was mean, Hunter. But I have a two-eyed jack to replace the piece."

"Sorry, but it is part of the game. Here's my move."

"Hunter, I have another two-eyed jack to complete a second sequence. I have won the game."

"I don't even have four in a row yet. What a drubbing."

"As you said, it is the luck of the draw."

"Memory, we should listen to the radio to see what is happening with the investigation of Foster's death. Oh my god. They just found professor Kenzo Lockwood from the medical school dead in his house. They think he died two days ago when Foster was killed. Cause of death has not been determined yet. Did you know this person?"

"This is really bizarre. Foster, Lockwood, and I have a joint $25 million research grant. It sounds like we are rich, but this money is to pay the costs of running the grant. All I get is two months' summer salary and travel money each year. We are furthering Randy Prather's fundamental research on one of the major breakthroughs of our time. When pig cells, tissues, or organs are transplanted into a primate, preexisting antibodies on the cell surface and the cell tissues or organs are immediately rejected. In 2001, his laboratory worked with Immerge BioTherapeutics and performed somatic cell nuclear transfer with cells in which they knocked out one allele of GGTA1. With this groundbreaking work, they were able to produce the world's first pig with a specific gene disrupted.

"Just recently for the first time, surgeons replaced a human heart with a pig heart in a living human. Even though the patient lived only two months, this is a major advance for medicine. Prather should receive the Nobel Prize for this achievement.

"But this raises disturbing questions. Disk and his friends may have been trying to get rid of all three of us on this grant. But I cannot imagine why. That means I am in even more serious danger.

I certainly cannot return to the university until this is straightened out."

"This is not good, Memory. We now have three possible reasons that someone is trying to get rid of you. We need to be even more careful to protect you. I better keep my gun loaded so I can react quickly."

"We have four more pork chops for dinner, and we can finish the cake for dessert. I'll wrap the pork chops in foil and put them on the grill along with the kettle. Now, let me feed Maple. Up here, Maple, time for dinner. Now go back to your corner where I left you some Cheerios."

"Hunter, the pork chops are done. I gave us a mug of milk and put the cake out. Nice meal and cleaning up is easy. Let's have a mug of coffee.

"Hunter, it is really hot in here tonight. Let's put Maple on her leash, take the blankets outside, and sleep on the ground. We can look at the stars."

"Memory, that's a good idea. I'll get Maple, and you gather up the blankets."

"Hunter, I'll put trash bags under the blankets to keep them clean. We can tie Maple to one of the porch posts. Now we can look at constellations. Do you know many?"

"Not many, Memory."

"My grandparents and I used to sleep outside sometimes, and we'd observe and discuss the constellations until I would fall asleep. See that W or M in the sky? That is Cassiopeia in the northern sky. In Greek mythology, the mother of Andromeda was a vain queen named Cassiopeia. She was placed in the sky as punishment for angering Poseidon by boasting of her daughter Andromeda's beauty.

"Before sunrise, I will show you Orion, the Hunter, which is a prominent constellation located on the celestial equator. You can spot Orion by looking for the three stars that make up his belt. The constellation below Orion's feet is Lepus, meaning 'hare' in Latin. Orion has two dogs chasing the hare. Orion's 'Greater Dog' constellation contains the brightest star in the sky called Sirius in Latin, or 'Dog Star.'"

"Memory, do you know the difference between a rabbit and a hare? Hares are born with fur and their eyes open, and rabbits with no fur and eyes closed. The astronauts are up there someplace."

"Hunter, as you know, my memory has a mind of its own. *Astronaut* is a compound word derived from the two ancient Greek words *astro*, meaning 'star,' and *naut*, meaning 'sailor.' So *astronaut* literally means 'star sailor.'"

"Another surprise, a TI-83 calculator has six times more processing power than the computer that landed Apollo 11 on the moon."

"That's incredible, Memory."

"We better go to sleep, Hunter. You need a lot of rest."

"Memory, you are thrashing about. What happened?"

"I got an earworm, Hunter."

"What is that, Memory?"

"That is when you have a song playing over and over in your head and can't stop it."

"So what song is in your head, Memory?"

"*Against the Wind* by Bob Seger. It is the story of someone who spent his life 'running against the wind.' I like it because I spend my whole life running against the wind."

"You certainly have, Memory. Can you go back to sleep now?"

"Maybe, Hunter. If we cuddle, it will help. But if you get handsy, I will move inside."

"Memory, get back under the blanket, and let's spoon."

"I have never been this close to a male before. It is a soothing feeling."

"Me too. I have never been pressed against a female before. It is an indescribable feeling. Sleep well, Memory. Have good dreams about me."

"Why do you think I am going to dream about you, Hunter?"

"Because I am irresistible, Memory?"

"You certainly think you are, Hunter."

"Perhaps I am just prescient, Memory?"

"Nice word. Good night, Hunter."

"Good night, Memory."

19

Joining Forces

Wow. That was an unforgettable experience lying next to Hunter. I have never been closer to anyone in my whole life. But is this just the result of our bizarre circumstance? Is it real? Is this the definition of love? Wanting to be together every minute, always supporting each other, doing everything for each other, and feeling free to tell intimate secrets to your partner? What more could anyone want? Why hasn't he proposed? And if he does, will I accept? Has he changed his mind? Is he afraid to ask? Should I ask him? Since I know his thoughts, I should leave it up to him. Hunter is up.

"I don't want this to end, Memory. Do we really have to get up?"

"Hunter, I am impressed at how well behaved you were last night. I wasn't sure you could do it, but we do need to start the day. I will bring Maple inside and feed her. She must be starving since I forgot to feed her last night. You bring the blankets inside and then make coffee, eggs, and toast for breakfast."

"Memory, let's eat outside. While we are eating, tell me something I don't know."

"Most people think that Mount Everest is the tallest mountain in the world. This is not true. It is the highest mountain in the world. The tallest mountain is actually Mauna Kea in Hawaii, which is more than a mile taller than Everest but shorter above sea level since 19,700 feet of it are under water in the Pacific Ocean."

"Probably most people don't know that, Memory."

"Now you tell me something I don't know, Hunter."

"Sheep can self-medicate. They use plants and other substances that otherwise hold no nutritional value to them to prevent or treat disease and teach their young to do the same."

"Hunter, I didn't know that. What are we going to do this morning?"

"Memory, I have something we need to talk about. I want to marry you."

"I was wondering how long it would take you to ask, Hunter."

"How did you know I was going to ask you to marry me?"

"When you had a fever, you proposed, but when you woke up you couldn't remember it. Do you really want to marry a murderer?"

"I think it would be exciting to marry a murderer, Memory. Never a dull moment."

"That sounds sick. Should I be scared of you?"

"Memory, you are the murderer, not me."

"Point taken! But I don't see me living on a ranch and raising sheep."

"My ranch is only twenty-five miles from the university. It's an easy commute. And killing sheep is a lot safer than killing people."

"What are we going to do for excitement, Hunter?"

"We can write a book about your story. I have already started writing it. I have the beginning of the book folded up in my back pocket."

"Hunter, all you wrote was the title: 'Memory' Survival. With this much writing, I'm surprised you didn't get carpal tunnel syndrome. That is a weird title."

"We have time to find a better title, Memory."

"Hunter, do you want to have kids?"

"One day I want to have a kid, but one day may be all I can take."

"Me too, Hunter. Anyway, if we had kids they would certainly be spoiled."

"Memory, all kids smell that way."

"Duly noted. Dorsa says marriage is like deleting all the apps on your phone except one."

"Memory, I would rather think of it as adding the most important app to your laptop. You are the last thing on my mind at night and the first thing on my mind in the morning."

"It's the same for me, Hunter."

"Actually, we have been together every day for quite a while. We may already have a common-law marriage."

"Hunter, they abolished common-law marriage in Missouri in 1921."

"You are just a wealth of happy information, Memory."

"Hunter, we have never even kissed."

"When I changed your bandage, I kissed your butt, Memory."

"I thought you had just drooled. What about sex?"

"Well, in France, if you hire a prostitute, you have to pay extra to kiss her. If kissing makes you nervous, we can make love without kissing."

"Hunter, did you just compare me to a prostitute?"

"For someone who is a twenty-three-year-old virgin, I thought you would be flattered."

"What happens if we don't like it?"

"Memory, I did not like eggs when my mother first served them, but eventually I learned to love them."

"So now you are comparing me to an egg, Hunter."

"Why does the word *laid* come to mind, Memory?"

"Hunter, so we will get up each morning and sit around the table having coffee and eggs together."

"We can go catfish noodling if you prefer, Memory."

"What kind of a wedding will we have?"

"Luckily, you can hire 'friends' on the internet, Memory."

"What are we going to do for a honeymoon, Hunter?"

"Running from the police works. We may have to honeymoon in a country without extradition."

"I won't take your last name, Hunter, since my research papers must all have the same name."

"No problem, Memory. You don't even know my last name. It is Stewart, by the way."

"Marriage is so permanent, Hunter."

"So is ink, but you still use your pen."

"Hunter, what is the secret to a happy marriage?"

"Live each day as if it were your last and each night as if it was your first. Are you stalling?"

"This is a big decision, Hunter. It is like buying a new laptop."

"That could be a little overstated, Memory. It is not that big a decision."

"Sorry, I was just bantering with you. Of course, I will marry you. But I have one condition: you must say 'I love you' ten times a day."

"If I don't say 'I love you' ten times before you finish brushing your teeth in the morning, you can have an amicable divorce."

"Hunter, did you have to bring up brushing your teeth again? What is an amicable divorce?"

"You keep your laptop and I keep mine. We should have our first kiss. Should we practice on Maple?"

"Hunter, the average person has their first kiss at fifteen, and it lasts ten seconds."

"Of course, you would know that, Memory."

"Let's hug and have our first kiss, Hunter."

"That was amazing, Memory. We need to do that often."

"Incredible feeling, Hunter. Yes, we need to do this often. We need to listen to the radio. The news just came on. There is nothing new about the two murdered professors. The police are still asking for tips, and I am now a person of interest in three murders. Oh no. The police have decided I could not have gone too far by horse, so they are going to use ATVs to scout the area near the slaughterhouse. This is a disaster. It will not take them long to find me. What can we do?"

"We could go to my place, Memory."

"But then they will arrest you for harboring a criminal. Also, we could run into anything along the way since my picture is probably everywhere."

"Memory, we might as well admit they are going to find us. So let's go on with life normally. You can use up the rest of the morning practicing martial arts, and I have paperwork to do for my research with the university."

"Good, Hunter. This is strenuous enough that it takes my mind off my situation. I will just keep going."

"That used up the morning, Memory."

"Hunter, we can have sandwiches for lunch. I will feed Maple, and you make the sandwiches. I will have ham and cheese, no mayo."

"Maple, I will feed you your bottles while you are standing. You are getting heavy."

"I made the sandwiches, and we have a little pasta salad left. It is on the plates outside."

"I like sharing everything with you, Hunter. How about you?"

"Memory, I never knew life could be so rewarding. I am so glad I met you. I have something else I want us to talk about. As I told you, I have a research appointment in the agricultural school and have a $5 million grant joint with Faith Finbar in the medical school to do sheep research. We have money in our grant to hire consultants, and we desperately need help with the computer science and mathematics. I want to hire you as a consultant on the grant. This will allow us to work together every day. And when we renew the grant, you can be an equal partner."

"That sounds exciting, Hunter. I love doing research, and doing it with you will be even more rewarding. What are we going to do this afternoon?"

"Memory, let's clean up, then take Maple to the pasture and let her run around. Put on your cowboy boots and hat. We can fill the water jugs while there. She will be safe with the horses. I'll put on her leash, and off we go. You open the gate, and I'll let her in. Wow! Maple is rubbing noses with Horse. While Maple gets exercise, we can do some bareback riding. We can ride around the outer edge of the pasture, and I will tell you some things about horses you do not know."

"Sounds great, Hunter."

"Okay, Memory. The speed at which they move is called a gait. Horses have four speeds: walking, trotting, cantering, and galloping. Horses generally gallop at around twenty-seven miles per hour. Horses begin trotting within hours of birth."

"I didn't know that, Hunter."

"People often call baby horses ponies. This is false. Baby horses are called foals, while a pony is just a smaller breed of horse. Also, horses and bunnies have in common that they cannot throw up or they will die since it goes directly into their lungs."

"Hunter, Maple is chasing us around. She is having fun. Tell me more."

"You can get a rough estimate of a horse's age by its teeth. Horses have baby teeth called milk teeth. Over time, they shed their milk teeth and get adult teeth that are longer and very concave. Over time, these teeth flatten down. Once a year, their teeth have to be 'floated.' This is the removal of sharp points from the cheek side of the horse's upper teeth and from the tongue side of the lower teeth. Most horses live about 30 years or more."

"I did not know that. Hunter, that was a relaxing and distracting afternoon. Let's fill the water jugs. It won't be easy grabbing up Maple since she is having so much fun here, but she still needs to be fed yet again. So we need to take her home. It will take two of us to corner her. I have her.

"You are okay, Maple, you just need to go home. Here's your leash. Hunter, you carry the water jugs, and I'll open the gate, and we are off. You are home, Maple."

"Memory, I feel well, so I will make rice and baked beans for dinner tonight. This is a complete protein meal, like meat or soybeans. In fact, on Rawhide, the cook, Wishbone, served beans almost every day. Let me put the rice in a pot on the grill. I will cut the top off the can of beans and put the can on the grill. When the rice is done, I will add the beans."

"I will feed Maple while you're doing that. Here, Maple, come get your dinner."

"Memory, dinner is ready. We can eat at the picnic table. The rice and beans are in one pot. You can scoop it onto your plate."

"I normally don't like rice, Hunter, but this mixture is good."

"Memory, tell me more about your eidetic memory."

"Another annoying thing about this weird memory is that I can't watch a rerun on TV. As soon as I see the title I can play the whole program in my head, skipping over the uninteresting parts."

"Why is that annoying exactly?"

"Well, people seem to like watching their favorite movies over again, but when I try to watch something again, it is irritating, knowing everything they are about to say before they say it."

"Does the same thing happen with books?"

"I don't reread books."

"What activities are the most fun for you?"

"Learning new things, creating sketches, composing music, doing math research, talking to new people, traveling to new places, eating new things, and probably a lot more things I've not tried yet. Since you have been behaving yourself, we'll sleep together again tonight so I don't have nightmares. But don't press your luck."

"I have to admit that the two lumps in my back were distracting last night."

"Hunter, what did you think they were?"

"I had a dream that a horse was pushing me from behind."

"So now you are comparing me to a horse."

"At least I didn't try to ride you, Memory."

"Do you not want me to push up against you, Hunter?"

"Maybe you could push harder, Memory."

"You just can't control your mind, can you, Hunter?"

"Memory, my thoughts are better than real life. Who gets on top tonight?"

"Hunter, you know full well we sleep side by side. You are pressing your luck."

"Not touching you requires more than luck. It requires overwhelming restraint."

"Hunter, I thought I heard you moaning last night."

"Actually, I was purring, Memory."

"This has gone far enough. Good night, Hunter."

"Good night, Memory."

"MEMORY" SURVIVAL

"Memory, I am getting crushed."

"That's because Maple jumped into bed with us. Her hoofs are really hard on the body. I will put her on the floor. We better switch to the top bunk. We will have to put the stuff from the top bunk under the bottom bunk. Now we are safe."

"Good night, Memory."

"Good night, Hunter."

20

Dodging Danger

Maple just woke me up. She should be starving. I forgot to feed her at midnight since I was so comfortable next to Hunter.

"Don't drink so fast, Maple. Sorry I forgot to feed you last night. Here, I will give you some extra Cheerios."

It's early blackberry season, so I can go pick some for breakfast. I have sugar and Bisquick to make blackberry cobbler. Let me start the oven's lower firebox and put a kettle of water on the grill. I will bring the stockpot to carry the blackberries in. It is foggy and cooler today. The blackberries are perfectly ripe. Now back to the cabin and make blackberry cobbler. This is simple. Put it in the oven. Hunter is up.

"Good morning, Wishbone."

"You just could not resist, could you, Memory."

"I think you slept well last night, Hunter. I had a terrible nightmare. Someone drove a car through the door of the cabin, jumped out with an axe, and I just made it out of bed before the axe swung into the bed. I ran behind the table, and they swung the axe into the table. It got stuck, so I ran to the shutters and took out the two-by-four as a weapon. Then I woke up. For some strange reason, they seemed familiar."

"That's a disturbing nightmare. I slept well, and it felt good. You were amazing last night, Memory. Imagine what it would be like if it was not just in my dreams."

"So you cannot control yourself even in your dreams, Hunter."

"MEMORY" SURVIVAL

"I can't help it. In the nighttime I sleep dreaming of you, and in the daytime, I dream of sleeping with you."

"Hunter, a proposal is not a license to have your way immediately."

"I was just hoping to get a head start on our wedding night, Memory."

"So you think our wedding night is going to make all your dreams come true. Don't count your chickens before they hatch, Hunter. What if I am not any good at it?"

"You are excellent at everything, Memory. Have faith in yourself."

"This is not like learning a new theorem, Hunter."

"Maybe it is. You just practice until you get it right, Memory."

"You are getting pretty far ahead of yourself, Hunter."

"I just don't want to be left behind, Memory. What happens if I am not good at it?"

"There is no chance you are going to be left behind, Hunter. You have practiced this so much in your mind you may be a world authority. You are already too far ahead of the curve."

"Are you talking about your wonderful curves, Memory?"

"Hunter, are you really going to start this first thing in the morning? Do I need to duct tape your mouth?"

"Sorry, I'll let it go. What do I smell?"

"I made us a blackberry cobbler for breakfast. It will be done shortly. Here is a mug of coffee to get you started."

"Memory, while we are waiting, tell me something interesting I don't know."

"Try this. Although Antarctica is made up of ice in the form of glaciers, ice shelves, and icebergs, it is classified as a desert because a desert is a landscape where little precipitation occurs and so living conditions are hostile for plant and animal life. It is actually the coldest, windiest, and driest continent. You can add to this the fact that 3 percent of the ice in Antarctic glaciers is penguin urine."

"Yes, that is interesting."

"The cobbler is done. Come to the table. We can have milk with it, and there will be enough left for tomorrow."

"Nice breakfast, Memory. I will clean up."

"I think I will open the shutters. Hunter, there is a dog outside."

"This is not good. Do you see his owner?"

"No."

"Let me go out and get the dog. He has a collar. His name is Dodger. This means he may also have a pet tracker, which will bring his owners straight to us. We need to get him out of here, but first, let me get the drone and search our surroundings. I will put Maple's leash on the dog and tie him to the porch post. Now, you carry the drone, and I will carry the controller."

"Hunter, how do you fly a drone?"

"We have a controller with two sticks. To increase speed, push the left stick forward, and to decrease speed, pull it backward. To go left, push the right stick to the left, or push it to the right to go right. Rotating the drone left or right is done by pushing the left stick to the left or right. This drone has a camera, and the controller has a viewer. I will hover over the area south of us looking for people. Then east, north, and west of us. I don't see anything. I will bring it home. To be safe, stay alert while it lands. There, we are done."

"It is interesting to see how a drone works, Hunter."

"Now I need to get this dog out of here. I will tie him off in the back of the ATV and take him to Boone County Animal Rescue. I'll bring back the leash. The police are searching for you east of us. So I will go west and then south to my ranch, then drive to the shelter. You need to stay inside with the door locked in case someone shows up. If someone knocks on the door, just don't answer it. While at my place I'll get some stuff we can use. See you soon."

I need to keep busy while Hunter is gone. I am too upset to do research or sketch. I can play my piano for a while and then practice martial arts inside. It will use up the time. Now I should feed Maple.

"Come here, Maple. Time for lunch. Luckily, you are very cute since you really are a lot of work. Hunter is at the door. Hi, Hunter. No one showed up."

"I brought back the leash, more straw to replace Maple's bedding, hay for Maple and the horses, ice, lunch meat, pasta salad, canned baked beans, milk for Maple, bread, and eggs. I also brought a change of clothes for me, toiletries, and changed my wound dressing while at the ranch. Let me take this stuff inside."

"Hunter, I am starving. Let's eat sandwiches and pasta salad for lunch."

"Nice lunch, Memory. I'll move the ATV behind the cabin. Now let me change Maple's straw and give her some more hay. I can throw the old next to the cabin. I have something I have always wanted to show you."

"I've seen it, Hunter!"

"I meant I got a College of Agriculture, Food, and Natural Resources Exceptional Alumni award. It is under the seat of the ATV. I will bring it in sometime."

"Sorry, knowing you, I thought you were about to take your clothes off."

"I'm worn out. Why don't you take the hay to the horses? It will give you a chance to drive the ATV. Here's the key."

"I'll take the water jugs to be filled."

Driving the ATV is nothing like I imagined. It has handlebars like a bike but six tires. It rides really rough. I'm at the pasture.

"Hi, horses. Here is some more hay. I can't stay, Hunter needs me. Let me fill the water jugs, and I am off."

Head back to the cabin.

"Hunter, that is quite a driving experience. That thing really pounds the ground."

"Yeah, it's not for the faint of heart. We need to listen to the radio. Not good. The police have found out that you have a joint grant with Foster and Lockwood. Worse, the coroner says that Lockwood also died of a broken neck. This makes you a person of interest in three murders. The police are confused as to what is happening. They seem to be stumped at the moment, but they definitely are running a full court press to find you.

"Memory, I would like us to spend all afternoon having a serious face-to-face discussion about our future. The divorce rate in the US is fifty percent, and it is sixty percent for people who get married between the ages of twenty and twenty-five. There is a divorce in the US every forty-two seconds. The biggest cause is 'unrealistic expectations.' That is because people don't sit down and discuss their idea of a future before they get married. Instead, they think their life is going to be a continuation of this current whirlwind love affair. Later, their life together is not what they thought it was going to be and they drift apart. The good news is that one of the lowest divorce rates is amongst farmers. We got together under very unusual circumstances, which puts us at risk. So I would like us to sit down with notepads for an hour and each write out what we want for our future. Then we can compare notes to see if we are both headed in the same direction."

"That is a wonderful idea, Hunter. See, you are also quite brilliant. Let's sit at the table."

"We are safe from most of the pitfalls of marriage. Money is a constant sore point in relationships. We both have big incomes, so we will not have that problem. Another problem is 'lack of equality.' We both have advance degrees, so we are immune to that problem. Children from divorced families have a higher divorce rate. We also do not have that problem. Other causes are domestic violence and alcohol, which we certainly do not have any problem with."

"You have really researched this, Hunter. I am glad that outside your bantering you are going to take marriage very seriously. I will. Thank you. Let's sit and write."

"That was an hour, Memory. Let me start my list by stating a fear. You have spent every minute of your life doing research, and I have spent every minute of mine running the ranch. Are we prepared to cut those activities in half so we can spend the other half together? I certainly am."

"Hunter, I spend all my time doing research since I have no one to share my life with. This did not necessarily make me happy. I would love to spend loads of time with you."

"On my list, Hunter, I want us to share the household duties: cooking, cleaning, laundry, shopping, etc. This then becomes together time."

"I completely agree, Memory. We can do some research together on my grant, but you certainly need time to do your own research. I would like us also to work together on the ranch on weekends so we can share this important part of our lives."

"For sure, Hunter. I would like an art studio and a music room."

"I have seen your sketches, Memory. Just one more thing you are gifted at. We can easily expand the ranch house to accommodate all space demands. We will each need an office with computer space, a big desk, shelves, etc."

"Hunter, I would like us to have separate bathrooms so we both can leave our stuff on the counter."

"Certainly, Memory."

"It would be nice if we have a spa room with a jetted tub so we can have tub parties, which you have clearly already fantasized about, Hunter."

"Definitely a requirement, Memory."

"Hunter, I am nervous about being around the ranch hands since I don't know them."

"You will be completely safe around them, Memory. They know how much I love you and so already love you also. They will lay down their lives for you. I would like for neither of us to make major decisions alone. We should both have input here."

"Clearly, Hunter. I would also like for us to tell our partner of any problems we are having. People often keep problems to themselves thinking they are saving their partner from grief. What usually happens is, problems cause subtle changes in behavior, which leaves the other person very uncomfortable."

"I agree, Memory. We are both mature enough to deal jointly with problems."

"Hunter, for holidays, birthdays, etc., I would like us to buy our favorite gift for ourselves. We can have it wrapped and give it to the other person to give us at the appropriate time. This way, we will always get the gift we want."

"That is fine, Memory. I think we need to keep separate bank accounts. We can set up one joint account to pay for housing and related joint bills. I will have to keep the current account for the ranch since it is necessary for tax purposes."

"That sounds good, Hunter. I would like you to stay near me when we go out in public. I have trouble doing small talk and have absolutely no idea when a male is coming onto me."

"I certainly will, Memory. You are stunningly beautiful and will attract all males within 500 miles. You will be much safer if we make it clear to everyone that we are inseparable. Neither of us seems to drink much. But at parties I will often take a drink so I do not look judgmental."

"Me too, Hunter. Another thing, I would like it if you would not sex banter in public. It would make me very uncomfortable."

"Actually, Memory, I have never done this in public. I designed it just for us."

"I would like us to have time to cuddle and watch TV some nights, Hunter."

"Definitely we need cuddle time, Memory. Neither of us has pets. We should leave it at that for now while we develop a schedule."

"Seems good, Hunter."

"You need to travel, Memory. We have enough money to travel together, and I can arrange to visit agriculture departments while you are in the math or computer science department."

"I was hoping you would say that, Hunter. There is one last thing that I think is critically important. Couples frequently get into arguments because one person has something bothering them and they spring it on their partner. Their partner didn't know there was a problem, has not had time to think about it, feels attacked, gets defensive, and then gets angry. Then things are said that should not be, and everyone is unhappy later on. I have read much literature on this, and there are two excellent approaches to problems. First, if the problem is not serious, like, 'Could you not leave your shaving cream on the bathroom sink? It does not leave room for me and my morning stuff. There is room in the medicine cabinet for it.' Even this is not the correct approach.

"A better approach: 'I have a problem I want to discuss. Is this a good time?' Then the other person can say 'Yes' or 'I am dealing with another problem right now. Can we meet at 7 p.m. tonight to go over it?' For serious problems, I want us to have a 'resolution book.'

If someone has something serious to discuss, instead of springing it on your partner and making them defensive, you put it in the resolution book and date it. Then your partner has time to read it, adjust to it, think about it, and then respond to it in the book. It is best if things are phrased in the resolution book as 'I want' or 'I feel' instead of 'You did.' Then we can sit down together and see if the proposed resolution works or if we need to adjust it."

"That is a great idea, Memory. I definitely will use the resolution book. I put on my list that I do not want kids right away, but I am not counting it out in the future."

"Me too, Hunter. I want us to have time to be together without interruption. After we establish a lifestyle, we can decide if we are fit to be parents."

"I completely agree, Memory. I should get a vasectomy so you do not have to put up with the side effects of birth control pills. It can be reversed later if necessary."

"As usual, that triggers my memory, Hunter. Did you know that pregnancy tests date all the way back to BC 1350. An ancient papyrus reports that Egyptian women urinated on wheat and barley seeds to determine if they were pregnant. If wheat grew, it not only predicted pregnancy, but also that the baby would be a girl. If barley grew, it predicted a male baby. If nothing grew, the woman was not pregnant. This system was surprisingly accurate. Experiments in 1963 showed that this system was accurate seventy percent of the time."

"That is amazing, Memory. Where do you want to be ten years from now?"

"What we just discussed our future to be but with less pressure on me to be a superstar at the university."

"Me too, Memory, and I would like the ranch to become completely independent so I have less pressure to keep it going forward. As far as I can see, we are on the same page about our future."

"We are certainly made for each other, Hunter."

"Memory, there is still leftover beans and rice we can have for dinner. We can have them cold."

"I need to feed Maple. I can get the milk out of the cooler and fill two bottles. Get up here, kid, and take your milk. Good girl. Get down and do your thing. I gave you some Cheerios."

"Memory, I put the rice and beans on the picnic table. Help yourself."

"Thanks, Hunter. We can eat and then clean up together."

"Hunter, I will sleep on your bunk again tonight, and we can just cuddle. If you get handsy, I will be on top. The top bunk, that is. As usual, we will have to sleep with our clothes on. Thank goodness for the fan."

"Memory, hop in, and let's spoon."

"I could grow to like this every night, Hunter."

"Me too."

"We should go to sleep before this gets out of control. Good night, Hunter."

"Goodnight, Memory."

21

Nothing Is as It Seems

"Time to get up, sleepyhead. You were well behaved last night. Thank you. I will feed Maple, and you can get breakfast. We can have Cheerios and milk for breakfast."

"Memory, the sun is up, so I'll put the bowls, spoons, Cheerios, and milk on the picnic table so we can listen to the birds and watch the squirrels."

"Sorry, Hunter. You know how my mind works. Everyone knows that the earth orbits the sun. But this is not true. Every object in our solar system exerts a gravitational pull on everything else. You can think of the solar system as a giant tug of war. As the celestial bodies pull against each other, a balance point is reached. At this point, all the forces of our solar system offset each other so it is stationary. This causes our solar system to orbit an invisible point at its center. This is called the barycenter and is the center of mass of the solar system which is the center of mass of every object in our solar system combined.

"This barycenter constantly changes position, depending upon where the planets are in their orbits. The solar system's barycenter ranges from being at the center of the sun to being outside the surface of the sun. It is around this point that the earth is orbiting, and even the sun is orbiting."

"I certainly did not know that, Memory."

"Tell me something I don't know, Hunter."

"An acre of wheat produces enough bread to feed nine thousand people for a day. One bushel of wheat can contain as many as ten million kernels. Wheat is one of the most produced crops on earth, using up over five hundred million acres."

"I didn't know that, Hunter. Let me open the shutters. Oh no! Birch, the head of the campus police, just arrived on a horse. Your ATV is behind the cabin, so he should not know you are here. He could be here to finish me off like Disk. Cover me with your rifle, and I will go out and talk to him."

"What are you doing here, Birch?"

"I came to tell you that you can come home, Dr. Holmes."

"People call me Memory, Birch. I don't trust you. Your partner tried to kill me. How do I know you're not here for the same thing?"

"I know that Disk tried to kill you, which is why I am here."

"How did you find me?"

"This is a complicated story. Can we go in and talk?"

"I don't feel safe around you with a gun."

"I will leave my gun in the saddlebags. Now, can we now go in and talk?"

"Yes, but you need to know that someone else is here and is armed."

"No problem. I am here to help."

"Come on in. This is Hunter. He owns the ranch west of here. Hunter, this is Birch, the head of the MU campus police. And this little lamb is Maple. Say baa, Maple."

"Hi, Birch. What's up?"

"Let's sit at the table and talk. This is a long story, so we might as well start at the beginning. After Disk was killed and the police listed you as a person of interest, I started asking around campus about you. I found out that you were the youngest full professor in the history of the University of Missouri and that on campus you are nicknamed Brain. I decided that you are probably clever enough to fake your death. So I started searching for you. After scouring the campus without success, I started searching the internet. There is a ton of information about you, but I did not get any hint as to where you might be.

"Then I decided that I needed to learn more about Disk since he was at the center of this. So I went over his employment records. I knew he came from the Chicago Police Department, and I decided to contact them to see what they knew about him. He had letters of recommendation from three retired officers in the department. But to my surprise, none of them had ever heard of Disk, and he'd never worked for the Chicago Police Department. He faked the letters of recommendation but used real names of people there, so it would not be obvious he had faked the letters. There was a risk that someone would contact one of these people, but he must have decided to take it.

"This made me really start looking deeper into what was going on. I reviewed Disk's records and saw that he had picked up one of your students several times over weekends, and later, she died by suicide. I contacted the counseling center, and since I'm the head of campus security, they told me under the table that she had been sex trafficked. This made me suspicious of whether Disk was running a sex trafficking ring on campus. Your roommate, Dorsa, seemed very concerned about you, so we met regularly to discuss my investigation. She made it clear that you were sure that Disk was probably sex trafficking. It wasn't too hard to figure out from there what was going on. You were investigating Disk for sex trafficking, and when he found out, he decided to get rid of you. So he must have come to your apartment with the gun we found in the trash, and you protected yourself with martial arts."

"Yes, but I did not intend to kill him. Because of an overload of adrenaline, I kicked him harder than I intended. Why did you come to my apartment that morning?"

"Actually, I was driving by and saw Disk's police car. Since he was off duty, he should not have been there in a police car. So I stopped to see what was going on. I ran inside your apartment building. Your door was open, and Disk was dead on the floor in the entryway. I dialed 911 and then saw your picture on the wall, so I ran outside looking for you. I saw you leaving and tried to follow, but I had a flat tire. So I ran inside and got Disk's car fob and took off after you."

"You figured out the whole situation. This is all true, but how did you find me?"

"Your school records had your grandparents as next of kin, so I went to interview them. They vehemently denied knowing if you were alive or where you were. I made a records search, but there were no properties in your name or your grandparents' names, except where they lived. Then I remembered that I saw their framed marriage certificate on the wall when I was there, and it gave your grandmother's maiden name. A search showed she owned this property with a log cabin on it. I assumed you were here. So I went to the agriculture school and got a horse and trailer. I parked north of here and rode the five miles to the cabin."

"Birch, one day a helicopter was overhead. Was that the police looking for me?"

"Yes, Memory. They were looking for any hint of you and any horses in the wilderness. But never did see anything."

"We have two horses, but when we heard the helicopter, we quickly moved the horses next to the cabin under the oak trees. What about the two professors who were murdered? Do you know what happened?"

"The police are still stumped, as am I, Memory. We cannot find any reason for this to happen, which makes it almost impossible to find the perpetrator. The police do not think you killed those two professors, but because of your connection to them, they want to talk to you. It is possible that all three of you on the grant were targets. But why?"

"I don't know why, Birch. So what should I do?"

"I told the police and the university what I found out. You can return since they know you are innocent. However, someone is killing off professors. They are connected to you somehow. So you may be in serious danger. You cannot just return to your apartment."

"I can stay at Hunter's ranch."

"But we still have to figure out how to keep you safe, especially on campus. I will assign a security guard to you."

"MEMORY" SURVIVAL

"Guys, I see Dorsa outside, and she is carrying a gun. Hunter, cover me with your rifle. You two hide, and I will go out to talk to her."

"Dorsa, how did you find me?"

"Birch and I met regularly while he was investigating you. He told me that there was a cabin in your maternal grandmother's name. It was not hard to find it online. Then I drove all around the outside of the property until I saw the rustic road coming in. Luckily, my Ford Explorer has four-wheel drive since I needed to make it up this rugged road. Then I walked in the last mile. Is this your horse?"

"Yes."

"Memory, are you alone?"

"Yes. Why do you have a gun?"

"I think you know."

"Dorsa, I really don't. I didn't even know you owned a gun."

"I kept it in the console of my SUV so no one would know I have it."

"I was right all along that Disk was sex trafficking on campus."

"You and everyone else missed the whole point. Disk was not sex trafficking. He was selling drugs, which is why he met with the students. I was the one sex trafficking. I ran up over $200,000 in debts at the casino that I owed to loan sharks and desperately needed money. I started the escort service to recruit girls and slowly transition them into prostitution. I then found out from my girls about Disk. So I approached him, and we went into business together. I paid him to give me the names of vulnerable female students."

"How stupid was I? It was obvious all along that it was you. I should have seen it the moment you made it clear that you knew more about sex trafficking than the university. Then you kept trying to stop me from informing the university. The only one of your dates I met dressed like a pimp. I should have realized that if you were losing money at the casino, you were in trouble. Also, it should have been obvious when Foster Brandon was found with a martial arts pin in his hand that you must have taken from my room. Then you left unusually early for work the day Disk tried to kill me. I had a nightmare that someone familiar was trying to kill me in the cabin.

I should have realized it was you. It was there right in front of me all along. Why didn't I see it?"

"Because of my psychology studies, I am very good at imitating a normal person."

"So why did Disk try to kill me?"

"You told me that you were going to contact the university on Monday about sex trafficking. I couldn't let that happen, so I told Disk you were going to turn him in. I left earlier than usual for school that Monday morning so Disk could get rid of you. It never crossed my mind you would kill him instead."

"How does this relate to the two professors who were killed?"

"Foster was divorced, and Kenzo's wife died of cancer, so they were using my escort service. Foster figured out that I was running a sex trafficking ring when one of my escorts accidentally gave me away. He then told Kenzo. They told me to close my operation, or they would turn me in to the university. I had no choice but to get rid of them. To throw more suspicion on you, I tasered them and then used a technique I saw on NCIS where they showed how the military kills with a neck snap. It is even easier to do when the person is incapacitated. You just have to turn the head very quickly 180 degrees. To point even more in your direction, I wore gloves and put one of your martial arts pins in Foster Brandon's hand."

"So what are you going to do now?"

"I cannot let you leave here and turn me in."

She knows that I know martial arts, so she will not get too close to me. But she does not know the spinning heel kick starts with your back to the person. So if I turn around, she will feel safe enough to come near me.

"There is something in the cabin you really need to see. Let's go in."

I will sign to Hunter to hit the floor and then do the spinning heel kick. Got her. Her gun went off. Luckily it missed me this time. Hopefully, no one was hit.

"Hunter, are you two okay?"

"We are fine. But she barely missed Maple. Birch used his cell phone to record Dorsa's confession. Is she dead?"

"MEMORY" SURVIVAL

"No. I just knocked her out."

"Coral, I will get my gun and handcuffs out of my saddlebags. Now we should all leave here. I will handcuff Dorsa, walk her to her car, and drive her to the police station. You two can go to Hunter's for now, but the police will probably have to talk to you. With my recording, they will know that you are completely innocent. Dorsa is awake and handcuffed, so let me take off, and you two take my horse to Hunter's. I will come by later and pick him up."

"Hunter, let's put Maple in her cage on the back of your ATV. We can ride to your ranch and pull the horse behind. I will sit on your lap. Let me grab my letter. There is a lot to be done here which we can take care of later. We need to bury the two boxes and bring the horses and other stuff from the cabin to your ranch. We will have to make several trips, but it can wait. I can't believe this nightmare is over and that Dorsa was the bad person all along. I was really fooled right from the beginning. It will be great getting back to civilization. Sometimes I wondered if I would ever have a normal life again. You saved my life. Thank you, thank you, thank you."

"Memory, so now we can get married and actually have a normal life."

"Hunter, I doubt we will ever have a normal life. On the other hand, we wouldn't like a normal life. But it might be relaxing for a while, anyway. As soon as we get to your place, I need to call my grandparents and tell them all is well. We're off."

22

The Beginning

"Memory, they said on the news this morning that an unusual fact about Maine is that it is the only state with a one-syllable name."

"Another unusual fact is that it is the closest point in the United States to Africa. Also, everyone knows that California has the longest shoreline of any state. But this is not exactly true. One can argue that Maine actually has the longest shoreline. This is because the National Oceanic and Atmospheric Administration (NOAA) has two measurements for shoreline. The first is the 'general shoreline,' which refers to the 'general outline' of a state's seacoast. It is the rough coastline, which includes shoreline with major bays and islands taken into account. For this shoreline, California measures 840 miles and Maine measures 228 miles. But NOAA has a second definition of shoreline, the 'tidal shoreline.' This includes 'shoreline of outer coast, offshore islands, sounds, bays, rivers, and creeks to the point where tidal waters narrow to a width of a hundred feet.' Under this measurement, California has 3,427 miles of shoreline and Maine has 3,478 miles."

"That is certainly a surprise, Memory."

"Thanks for coming to the bank with me, Hunter. My grandparents have signed over the safe deposit box to me. We can go in and open it. I put my key in the box, the teller puts her key in the box, and it opens. Let's see what's inside."

"MEMORY" SURVIVAL

"Memory, this is a statement from a stock brokerage. You are co-owner with your parents of two stocks. The first is three hundred shares of Amazon stock that your parents bought at $18 a share when the stock first went public in 1997 for an investment of $5,400. Since then the stock split, then split three to one, then split again, then split twenty to one. So you now have seventy-two thousand shares.

"Let me use my phone and see what they are worth today. Wow! It is selling at $135.64 a share."

"Oh my god, Hunter. After capital gains tax, this stock is worth $9,766,080. I can't believe it."

"Memory, just before they died, your parents paid $14,787 for three hundred shares of Google at $49.29 a share. Online it says that the stock has split twice and then twenty to one and is now selling for $115.25 a share."

"So my one thousand and two hundred shares are now worth $2,766,000, Hunter."

"Of course, you instantly computed this in your head, Memory."

"It comes with the territory."

"You are filthy rich, Memory."

"I don't feel any different."

"Does this make me a trophy husband?"

"Hunter, I already know you are wealthy. This just means that I am not marrying you for your money."

"So you are marrying me for my looks?"

"Which of your looks would that be, Hunter? We should pay off the mortgage on the ranch. How much is it?"

"Today, around $1,110,000. But the current price of farmland in Missouri is $3,000 per acre, so the 2,000 acres alone are worth $6 million."

"Hunter, I'll put these papers in my backpack. What are we going to do with all this money?"

"We do need a new thermos, Memory."

"You used a lot of brain power to come up with that, Hunter."

"Well, I don't want to spend the money all at once."

"Don't worry, I think you will have a little left over after that purchase. We can think about this another time. We need to go to my grandparents' house for the wedding."

"Memory, you are not wearing a wedding dress."

"Hunter, I have never worn a dress in my life. Can't you see that I am wearing your clothes? Besides, you are wearing your hunting clothes."

"Yes, but at least I left my gun in the car. My father is going to perform the wedding in sign language. He went online and got ordained so he could perform our wedding."

"Hunter, we are here at my grandparents for our wedding. You have known them a long time, but I have never met your parents. I don't even know their names. This is a little unnerving."

"My father's name is Jack, and my mother is LoVeta. Don't worry. I told them right at the beginning that I met the most perfect person in the world, that I was in love with and wanted to marry."

"I don't think this is going to be a typical wedding."

"Memory, this may be closer to a typical divorce."

"Does this mean we are going to have sex tonight?"

"Not just tonight. Every day and night, Memory."

"Pervert."

"Memory, you really like that word."

"It covers a multitude of sins, Hunter. Okay, I will try it once to see if I like it."

"Memory, what are you going to do if it becomes your favorite pastime?"

"Write fewer papers, I guess."

"And I will have to hire an extra person to run the ranch."

"Hunter, do you think we will be spending all day in bed?"

"Absolutely not. We will have to go to the kitchen to eat peanut butter sandwiches to keep up our strength."

"Hunter, there must be more to marriage than sex."

"Memory, we may have to buy the book *Sex and Marriage*."

"I think that is how to fit sex into marriage. We need a book on how to fit marriage into sex. We have never even seen each other naked."

"MEMORY" SURVIVAL

"Memory, we could go in the coat closet and play show-and-tell again. You can show and I won't tell."

"Birch sent us a wedding present in the form of a letter. It reads, 'I spent all day yesterday with the police, and they now know you are completely innocent. They don't really have to talk to you right now. Congratulations on your wedding. You are free.'

"Here comes my parents. Memory, did you just sign 'I am very happy to meet you' to my father?"

"Yes, and he signed back, 'You really are as special as Hunter said you are. You even went to the trouble to learn sign language.'"

"I know, and then you signed, 'Hunter is a very special person.' And he signed, 'We know that.'"

"Your mother signed that she is very happy we are getting married. I signed 'Thank you.'"

"I signed for Jack what my grandfather said: 'This is the first wedding ever held in our house.'"

"I signed, 'There have been nineteen weddings held in the White House, the latest being November 19, 2022, when Naomi Biden, the granddaughter of President Joe Biden, married Peter Neal on the south lawn. This was the only wedding of the grandchild of a president in the White House. James Buchanan is the only president to never be married in his lifetime. You can add to that the fact that some states have produced an inordinate amount of our forty-six presidents. Eight came from Virginia, seven from Ohio, and five from New York. Missouri had the thirty-third president of the United States, Harry S. Truman.'"

"Your father signed, 'Memory, you are just as knowledgeable as Hunter said you are.'"

"I will translate the wedding for my grandparents. We are ready to start."

"Jack's father signed, 'Dearly beloved we are here today to say goodbye to Hunter.'"

"LoVeta signed, 'Jackson, this is a wedding not a funeral.'"

"Jack signed, 'Is there a difference?'"

"LoVeta signed, 'Is that all you got out of thirty years of marriage?'"

"Jack signed, 'Plus a mortgage.'"

"LoVeta then signed, 'You'll be lucky if you don't also get to pay alimony.'"

"Jack signed, 'You know I'm joking.'"

"LoVeta signed, 'You hope I'm joking. Besides, we are not losing a son, we are gaining a daughter.'"

"Hunter, now I know where you got your bantering skills."

"Jack signed, 'Do you have rings?'"

"Hunter signed, 'We each have thumb drives on neck chains so the other person will have everything about their partner with them at all times.'"

"Jack signed, 'You two have written your own vows. So, Memory, do you take Hunter to be your lawfully wedded husband?'"

"I am signing: 'Hunter, I promise to keep our laptops synchronized for the rest of my life.'"

"Jack signed, 'And, Hunter. Do you take Memory to be your lawfully wedded wife?'"

"Hunter signed, 'Memory, I promise to worship the ground you walk on for the rest of my life.'"

"Jack signed, 'You may kiss each other. As strange as this is, I now pronounce you married.'"

"Hunter, you said that your parents and my grandparents are giving us a honeymoon for our wedding present. What is it?"

"Since you have decided to take a semester off from school to recover from this nightmare, they rented us a luxury log cabin just outside Vail, Colorado, for three months. At $1,000 per day, this is quite a present. The cabin is isolated on the side of a mountain, has fifteen rooms, an indoor pool and hot tub, a gym, and a massive kitchen. There are six TVs with cable and Wi-Fi. It is three stories, has three fireplaces, a wraparound porch, king-size beds, and the front is all windows with spectacular views. There is also a music room full of instruments and a grand piano and a library. There is a food delivery service. I told them we do not need to rent a car since all our traveling will be between the bedroom and the kitchen."

"Hunter, you actually said that to our families?"

"Yes, and if we like it, we could consider buying it for $5 million so all of us will have a place to vacation. We can hire a company to rent it out in the meantime. My parents will move into the farmhouse and run the ranch while we're gone. They will oversee the ranch hands emptying the cabin, burying stuff, and bringing the horses to the ranch. They will also empty your apartment. Dorsa's stuff can go into storage, and your things will be brought to the ranch. Then they will cancel the lease on your apartment."

"That's quite a leap from buying a thermos to buying a luxury log cabin, Hunter."

"But the average cost is not bad, Memory."

"Hunter, average doesn't really make sense in this setting."

"And they stocked the refrigerator with peanut butter sandwiches."

"You told them about this? How gross."

"They wanted to know why I packed almost no clothes for a three-month vacation. What was I supposed to tell them? Anyway, they had already gotten over the shock of learning that you are still a virgin."

"Hunter, you told my grandparents that I am still a virgin? Is there no limit to your perversions? Next you'll tell them you played with my butt."

"I told them that long ago, Memory."

"Hunter, my grandparents are not supposed to know about my sex life."

"They told me you were so advanced at age twelve that they gave you books on sex and birth control in case you started having sex in college. They did not realize it would actually have the opposite effect. They are rooting for you."

"Hunter, you have my grandparents rooting for me to have sex. Pervert. This is outrageous even for you."

"And my parents also, Memory."

"I am speechless, Hunter. Have you told the whole world? I hope that at least you did not tell the ranch hands."

"They were amazed at how disciplined we are. I also told the sheep, but they did not know what the word *virgin* meant."

"You really do have no limits. I am surprised you did not put it in the newspaper."

"I tried to, Memory, but they turned it down as being too racy."

"Hunter, have the five of you been planning out my sex life?"

"You weren't, and somebody had to. And five heads are better than one."

"After this, I expect our sex life to be our secret."

"Memory, I guess we can call off our twice-a-week meetings about you. We also have a private plane to take us to Vail."

"Does it have beds?"

"No, but if you are in a rush, I can rent a bigger plane."

"Don't press your luck, Hunter. In light of you telling the whole world about my sex life, you are lucky I am even going with you."

"I nearly bought out the pharmacy of condoms we can use until I get a vasectomy. The pharmacist asked, 'Do you want a bag?' I responded, 'No, she's not ugly.' After the pharmacist got over the shock, I took a bag since I had quite a load."

"You just couldn't resist, could you, Hunter?"

"We need to go to the airport, Memory. I have always admired that perfect mind, Memory. But when we are done with this honeymoon, I also want to know more about your body than you do."

"So do I need to bring graph paper, Hunter?"

"No. I expect to admire the world's most perfect combination of body and mind every day for the rest of my life. We are off."

About the Author

Peter Casazza and Janet Tremain are married and worked in the Mathematics Department at the University of Missouri–Columbia for forty years and then retired. They currently reside in Columbia, Missouri. They have written three hundred research articles and books in mathematics. While working as mathematicians, they traveled to thirty-five countries lecturing in mathematics.

They lived a year in Israel, two years in the United Kingdom, two years in Denmark, plus extended stays in Argentina, Austria, Belgium, Canada, China, France, Germany, Iceland, Italy, Luxembourg, Mexico, Morocco, the Netherlands, New Zealand, Poland, Spain, Sweden, and Switzerland. They kept in shape all those years with racquetball, squash, and cycling. They also had a large number of PhD students.

In their spare time, they enjoy swimming, art, music, cooking, hiking, reading, writing, woodworking, board games, cards, playing pool, and teasing each other. For twenty years they gave up three rooms of their house for "rabbit rescue" for the Central Missouri Humane Society housing over one hundred rabbits over this time.

They are still writing mathematical papers. Mathematical research requires exceptional creativity. So they decided to write a creative murder mystery/love story as a new challenge, and are already writing a sequel.

Printed in the USA
CPSIA information can be obtained
at www.ICGtesting.com
LVHW091811240823
756139LV00004B/420